For Jazmin
Enjoy!

Jordan Parkinson has enjoyed telling stories her entire life. Growing up on a farm with a large family taught her the importance of people and interconnectedness, which inspired her to go on to receive a Bachelor's degree in History with a minor in English. She has aspirations to eventually receive a Ph.D and to continue to learn about people and their lives, using storytelling as a bridge. She believes that the characters in her works, though fictional, are people she has to meet and get to know through the process of telling their stories.

For the real Donald:

Always

them, they shock me. They do things I hadn't planned on and make choices that make me so happy for them. They make choices that break my heart. Much of the time as I write, I feel as though I'm merely watching it play out: only the tool for a story that must be told.

One for My Baby has been an incredible experience for all of these reasons. Using people in my life as inspiration, I've been able to pour my entire soul into this work. Rosemary's story came to life before my eyes. Every beautiful and tragic moment, every sun-filled moment. It was a joy to get to know her and to get to know all of the other colorful characters. Their story is one of brokenness and tragedy. It is one of fear and hopelessness. It is one of despair. But it is also a story of true love and its overwhelming ability to conquer all of these things. It has been an honor to write.

—Jordan

One

Newport, Rhode Island
Summer 1954

Thomas Davenport introduced himself to her at a quarter to ten in the morning, a checkered cap scrunched in his hand. It seemed to happen by accident, and when it was over, Rosemary couldn't remember exactly what was said. She would learn rather quickly over the next weeks that this was the way of things with him: brief, exhilarating moments followed by cloudy recollections of a brilliant smile and admiral blue eyes.

There was something strange about him, something which left her feeling uneasy later. He had a way of pushing himself on people in the most charming way so that later one had no clue exactly what had occurred. But at the same time, he carried a magnetism that drew a person toward him and left them feeling oddly empty when he was gone. Or at least that's what he did to Rosemary.

She saw him approaching across the dock, weaving his way through the small crowd of them gathered to go yachting. She had heard of him, of course, before the season even began. The new, wealthy young man who had purchased the Carters' mansion would now be mingling

Jordan Elizabeth Parkinson

One for My Baby

Austin Macauley Publishers
LONDON · CAMBRIDGE · NEW YORK · SHARJAH

Copyright © Jordan Elizabeth Parkinson (2020)

All rights reserved. No part of this publication may be reproduced, distributed, or transmitted in any form or by any means, including photocopying, recording, or other electronic or mechanical methods, without the prior written permission of the publisher, except in the case of brief quotations embodied in critical reviews and certain other noncommercial uses permitted by copyright law. For permission requests, write to the publisher.

Any person who commits any unauthorized act in relation to this publication may be liable to criminal prosecution and civil claims for damages.

This is a work of fiction. Names, characters, businesses, places, events, locales, and incidents are either the products of the author's imagination or used in a fictitious manner. Any resemblance to actual persons, living or dead, or actual events is purely coincidental.

Ordering Information
Quantity sales: special discounts are available on quantity purchases by corporations, associations, and others. For details, contact the publisher at the address below.

Publisher's Cataloging-in-Publication data
Parkinson, Jordan Elizabeth
One for My Baby

ISBN 9781647502584 (Paperback)
ISBN 9781647502577 (Hardback)
ISBN 9781647502591 (ePub e-book)

Library of Congress Control Number: 2020917984

www.austinmacauley.com/us

First Published (2020)
Austin Macauley Publishers LLC
40 Wall Street, 28th Floor
New York, NY 10005
USA

mail-usa@austinmacauley.com
+1 (646) 5125767

after writing a few chapters, *One for My Baby* somehow got put on the back burner for a few years.

In the autumn of 2016, I picked up this book again and read over what I'd written years before. But the plot I'd had in mind wasn't reachable anymore. I just realized it wasn't quite right. But Rosemary wouldn't leave my mind, nor would the idea of this dying age.

So as I continued thinking about it, realizations came popping up into my head. I looked back on what had happened in my own life since I'd begun it. I thought of the people I'd met, the experiences I'd had. And I realized that Rosemary's story was still there, but different than I'd first thought.

I had always been fascinated with the idea of basing my characters off people I knew or at least knew of. I'd never done that before. But life had blessed me with many impactful people, and I realized the depth of this novel couldn't be reached without them. I began a character journal in which I wrote out each character: their fears, likes, dislikes. Everything from Donald hating tomatoes to Rosemary fearing that she'll never be worthy of true happiness.

As I worked on this character journal, I knew that some characters simply had to be based on certain people in my life. I interviewed some of these people and used what I knew of others, and eventually *One for My Baby* came to life on the pages. And for a long time, I couldn't decide how to end it. I couldn't decide what would be best for all of my characters.

But as a writer, I find that I'm constantly being surprised by the characters I write. Sometimes as I am writing about

Author's Note

In the summer of 2014, I sat in my home and watched the 1956 film *High Society* with Frank Sinatra, Grace Kelly, and Bing Crosby. As a long time and ardent Frank Sinatra fan, it wasn't uncommon for me to be doing that.

I remember watching this movie and being completely intrigued by the idea of life in Newport. By the 1950s, the traditional season was at its dying point. Many of the large families were selling their homes and changing their lifestyles. By the 1960s, Newport was no longer what it had been.

My mind began turning with ideas of what life in Newport was like around this time, right before the death of traditional high society. A character by the name of Rosemary Covington began surfacing in my mind. A young lady with a seemingly golden life who was secretly suffering.

I began working on this novel right away. I began working on who she was and what her life was like. I imagined that it would be a novella. A short look into the life of this fading world and a woman with her whole life ahead of her who felt just as faded. As fate would have it,

I would like to thank the wonderful people at Austin Macauley without whom this book would be gathering digital dust. I also want to thank the several family members and friends who made sure that the process of creation did not leave me insane.

with them during the summer months. At the first party of the season several weeks before, it seemed that everybody had already met him. Everybody except Rosemary. And for some reason, she had preferred it that way.

It had to do with that sort of uneasy feeling he evoked wherever he went. She had somehow felt it before she'd even met him. This was precisely why she pressed her red lips into a smile as he came unavoidably near, but did not remove her white sunglasses. She felt her fists clench at her sides, a nervous habit she usually tried to push away.

"I think you're the only one here I haven't met." He tilted his head when he spoke, and Rosemary would come to learn that it was normal for him to constantly look as though he was fighting a smile.

"It must be strange," she commented lightly. "Here you are coming to a place where you don't know a soul, and yet all of us think we know everything about you. You must get the feeling that you don't really have to meet anyone." He did smile then and chuckled a bit at her sense of humor. It seemed as though there was something he knew that she didn't, and very suddenly she wished that she knew what it was.

"If I have a reputation that precedes me then you must know that you do as well, Miss Covington," he answered, taking her offered hand for a brief moment and leaving it cold when he dropped it again. "I've heard that you are one of the only truly honest people left on the earth. And now I can see why your friends think that of you." Now it was Rosemary's turn to laugh softly.

"I would ask who could be saying such things about me, Mr. Davenport, but I have a feeling I already know," she nodded to him then. "Though it was a pleasure to formally meet you. Are you taking your own boat out today?"

"I'm afraid it isn't quite ready yet. It's a shame," he answered, pulling his cap over his dark hair and casting an inconvenient shadow over his eyes. "I'll be with David Merrill for the day and a few of the others. A great group of guys, if a bit too on the stick."

"I'd have to agree with you," she said, surprised he'd made her laugh again. It wasn't often she met a person as aware of the way they lived. Ophelia was, of course, but she was certainly different than Thomas Davenport. His statement that the men of this particular social circle were a bit too put together was refreshingly accurate.

"This your boat?" he gestured to the one nearest them, which was frantically being loaded with baskets of food and drink for the outing.

"A graduation gift," she said with a nod. "My father is extremely practical that way."

"You attended Radcliffe?" he asked casually, lighting a cigarette as he did so.

"Where else is there?"

"Journalism?" he turned his head a bit and blew out a puff of smoke before tossing the cigarette on the ground and stamping it out.

"Is it that obvious?" she answered, glancing curiously at the barely used cigarette. Perhaps he was one of the few in society who didn't really enjoy the common practice.

He surprised her by laughing before he answered, "Not really. I just thought it would be a pleasing bit of irony if you were a journalist. Seeing as though you're the only honest one left in the world."

"So they say." She had the urge to step away but disciplined herself. "What do you do with yourself when you're not in Newport being introduced to everyone, Mr. Davenport?"

"Business of some kind, I'm sure." He threw it out flippantly with a shrug of his shoulders, "I have a house in Havana that uses up my time."

It was at this point in their conversation that the others milling about the docks began piling into their separate boats, and the gang of guys with David Merrill began shouting for him to join them. He waved them off with a flashy grin and turned back to her, though he remained a bit turned away as if ready to spring toward the boats at any minute.

"Would you consider being friends, Miss Covington?" he asked, and somehow his candor didn't offend her. That, too, would become something she'd quickly learn about him.

"No, Mr. Davenport," she answered lightly. "It would be nothing but a disaster." Ever full of surprises, he smiled as if he'd known what she was going to say and trotted to where the others were waiting for him.

Two

"If you didn't bring gin, there isn't any point in being here." Ophelia was lounging back in the yacht, lazily blowing the smoke from her cigarette toward the ocean waves, the long holder perched in her hand. "I'll never understand why you gave it up, poor dear."

Rosemary couldn't resist a shake of her head, "If you don't drink, you never lose your head, Ophelia. Remember that. But yes, there is gin."

"Were you rude to Thomas?" Ophelia asked in response, the wide brim of her straw hat hiding her face as she dipped toward the cooler.

"Just honest," Rosemary answered, taking the water Ophelia offered her and smiling when her friend lounged back in her seat once again, positioning her small Chinese Crested in the crook of her free arm as she sipped her drink. His name was Ralph, and Rosemary honestly couldn't remember a time when he hadn't accompanied Ophelia almost everywhere.

"What a refreshing conversation it must have been," Ophelia remarked, setting her drink aside, her pink lips forming into a perfect smile. "You've finally met somebody just as honest as you."

"I'm not sure if he is as much honest as he is outspoken. And besides, you are very direct yourself. So I've no clue why you've gone around telling him stories about my so-called honesty."

"There's no need for that kind of pretense." Ophelia removed her large, dark sunglasses to reveal her sky blue eyes. "I am honest because I'm rich enough to get away with it. You are honest simply for the sake of being a genuine individual. It's simply exhausting and endearingly charming."

"You keep talking this way and I'll need some gin."

"You hate gin."

"Exactly." Rosemary couldn't help smiling at their banter, taking a sip of her water before settling back into her chair. Some time passed then, with nothing but the sound of waves and laughter from other boats, and the sharp smell of Ophelia's cigarette.

Soon they would head back to shore, each of them dispersing to their different mansions to get ready for dinner. They would gather in each other's homes, changed into suits and gowns while discussing politics or film. They would smoke cigarettes and drink champagne before and after a meal of lobster or steak, and some of them wouldn't make it home until the sky turned an orange shade of pink. And after some hours of sleep, the day would begin all over again. With the same people but different diversions. This was the life in Newport during the season, and this year it irked Rosemary more than usual.

She thought back again on her brief encounter with Thomas Davenport, and couldn't understand why it left her feeling simultaneously pleased and uneasy. She had to admit, his forthrightness was incredibly refreshing. She had the feeling that should she meet him over an evening of champagne and lobster, the conversation would be much more fulfilling than the usual tipsy arguments. *Brown vs. Board of Education of Topeka* was the latest hot issue and one that was either severely banned or openly debated.

But yet Rosemary also felt it strange, how Mr. Davenport seemed almost too comfortable in his own skin, as though he held a secret from the rest of the world. He seemed the type of person one would enjoy being around, and yet not entirely trustworthy.

"Have you noticed all of the people coming into town for the jazz festival?" Ophelia said, breaking Rosemary's thoughts.

"Oh, yes," Rosemary answered, trying to brush away the threads of irritation she now felt as a result of thinking too much. She disliked it when she was unable to figure something out. It didn't sit well when things couldn't seem to be given a particular explanation. However, hiding this from Ophelia was next to impossible.

"I assume that the festival isn't the reason you're suddenly upset. You'll go, of course?"

"Of course I will. Everybody's been talking about it for ages."

"But?" Ophelia prodded. "I thought if anybody, you'd be thrilled to attend." Rosemary finally looked over to see that her friend was watching her curiously, perhaps already knowing the answer that wasn't being put into words.

"Don't you find it all terribly ironic, Ophelia? We spend summers drinking and celebrating or attending festivals or charity balls, and we think we're helping humanity."

Ophelia was silent for a moment, looking out over the waves toward the other boats that were beginning to head back to shore. "Why does it seem to bother you more this year than any other?"

"It's just that everything is so predictable," Rosemary finally admitted. "We live this way because that's the way it is, yet there is never anything that I can look at and know for certain of its rightness. I can't seem to make sense of it."

Ophelia nodded briefly as though she understood, content to let the subject drop for now. But Rosemary shouldn't have been surprised that this conversation on the boat wasn't the last that she was to hear of the jazz festival that day. To be held in Newport Casino on Bellevue Avenue, it would be the first of its kind, and everybody was talking about it. Later that evening as she sat in her room arranging her hair, her mother came bursting in, maids trailing behind looking more like mountains of fabric than human forms.

They carried dresses, piles of dresses, all of which had been sent from designers in New York City or Paris for them to pick and choose which they'd prefer to wear to the big events of the season. The ones they didn't want would be sent back. But until that time, it seemed that June Covington was content to fling them about from room to room. "I've brought you options, my dear," June cooed, ordering piles to be displayed across various pieces of furniture.

"I've already chosen my gown for this evening, Mother."

"Well, it wouldn't do any harm to look again. Besides, there are also some lovely choices here for the jazz festival.

Or any of the other events for the season," June answered, seeming to separate simple evening gowns from more formal ball gowns to demonstrate her point.

"And if I weren't to go to the festival or the other events?" June recognized the teasing tone in Rosemary's voice right away, but it didn't stop her from furrowing her brow a bit.

"I suppose you really don't have to. Nobody is forcing you to be a part of society." Her mother's voice came off so light that Rosemary had to laugh.

"So you'll just take Hazel then?"

"It would seem so. Try to get to bed at a decent hour." June started pulling out different gowns then, clearly finished with their casual banter as she sent the maids out the door. Once finished with her hair—a beautiful construction of large auburn curls that swooped away from her forehead and pinned low near her neck—Rosemary joined her mother at the dress piles.

"How was yachting today?" June's voice was steadier now as she ruffled through dresses.

"Oh, fine," Rosemary answered absently, taking notice of pink chiffon reaching out from a pile of evening gowns. "I finally met Thomas Davenport."

"Did you?" There was no hiding the intrigue and curiosity in her mother's voice, which Rosemary couldn't help but smile at as she pulled the dress out.

"Yes. And before you jump to any conclusions, you should know that I don't approve of him." Rosemary carried the dress over to the mirror and held it in front of her. The sleeves were short and thin, made of only a few layers of chiffon. The skirt fell in loose folds from a tight bodice, whispering against the floor. Before even really surveying the dress in depth, Rosemary knew she wanted to wear it that evening, completely forgetting about her previous choice.

"Why is that?" June began shuffling through Rosemary's jewelry to find a piece that matched the gown.

"Something about him makes me uneasy." Rosemary draped the dress over a chair and went to find shoes. "I don't really understand why, but I don't entirely trust him." June was silent for a time, waiting as her daughter slipped into the dress and then quietly did up the row of buttons for her.

"Well, try not to make judgments that are too hasty," she finally said, clipping a bracelet studded in diamonds around Rosemary's wrist and then finally finishing with a necklace. "I know that you have sound judgment, Rosemary, and usually I trust your instincts. But when it comes to men, especially men near your age, you know it is harder for you to be objective," she spoke this as gently as possible, but still, an all-too-familiar raw feeling welled up inside Rosemary and her heart began to pound quickly. Strange, how fear could do that.

"Yes, Mother," she answered quietly, slipping into her shoes, spritzing perfume lightly across her neck, and taking the small clutch June handed her.

"Now, don't be down, darling." Mrs. Covington's eyes were soft, "Just keep it all in mind, that's all I'm saying. Will Mr. Davenport be at Ophelia's tonight?"

"It's more than likely."

"Well, put on some more lipstick on the way over, and smile. You look magnificent."

Three

Rosemary took her mother's advice and applied more lipstick in the short car ride over to Ophelia's. She held her compact steadily before her, the light pink lipstick gliding on effortlessly. She only wished her insides felt as steady and admitted that she could surely use a drink. Every so often, she had to remind herself exactly why she had given up the common practices of smoking or drinking, and she knew they were practical. First of all, she didn't need to depend upon anything to help her, and secondly, it all felt much too *in*. Rosemary tried to avoid following the actions of the crowd at all costs.

Though smoking hadn't been hard to give up. She'd hardly ever smoked before she had made the decision, and so giving it up completely hadn't been much of a challenge. However, it was moments like these of strange uncertainty, expectancy, and lingering pain from a resurfaced wound that reminded her how much a good bit of whiskey could help a person. Though what she had to fear or expect, she certainly didn't know.

For some reason, her mother's words had rattled her more than she would've admitted to anyone. She didn't like that there might be several other layers to Thomas

Davenport she couldn't see, and yet logically she knew there were. The entire thing almost made him seem even less trustworthy to her, while also forcing her to admit that perhaps she'd been too harsh in judging him. In any case, she understood that she had no reason to apologize for being exactly as she was. She hadn't said or done anything to him that she wouldn't have to anyone else. It was part of what made Rosemary who she was: that strange, consistent honesty.

The car slowly rolled onto the gravel of Ophelia's drive, creating a long crunching noise before it finally stopped in front of the grand entrance. The huge, white house was lit magnificently from the inside as if glowing with a terribly wonderful secret.

Rosemary left the comfort of the leather seats behind as she stepped from the car, and her heels made small clicking sounds as she walked up the marble steps that spilled off the front of the house. She could hear music playing softly from an upstairs window, probably Ophelia still getting ready for the evening. Rosemary had hoped to show up earlier than anybody else, and it sounded as though she had succeeded.

She didn't wait long once she reached the top of the stairs. The massive doors opened almost immediately after her ring, and she was greeted by the deep voice of Ophelia's butler Anthony.

"Hello, Miss Covington, please come in." He was a large man, tall with exceedingly broad shoulders and a ready smile that flashed brilliantly white against his black skin. He took her clutch, leading the way further into the ornate entryway. "Miss Baxter is still readying for the evening, though I'm to tell you that you are more than welcome to join her in her suite."

"Thank you, Anthony," Rosemary answered although she was already halfway up the marble staircase. From the top of its curve, it didn't take long to reach Ophelia's grand master suite. The main entrance was a tall, white door that led to a room of simple elegance. Ophelia was the only one Rosemary knew who could have a home that showed her endless wealth so gracefully.

"Ophelia?" Rosemary called, closing the door behind her.

"Oh, I was hoping you'd show up early!" Ophelia suddenly appeared from inside the closet, holding up two different gowns. "Which one?"

"Blue," Rosemary answered, settling herself on the nearby divan. She hummed to herself for a moment, one of her favorite songs, and almost wished she were back in her room with her records. She loved the time she spent getting ready for things because she could play her music and let it fill her soul. Somehow it always seemed to put things back where they belonged. She had been listening to her favorite music that night—Mr. Sinatra, of course—but her mother's arrival had quickly interrupted it. Ophelia must've heard the humming, as she quickly stuck her head back out of the closet.

"I should've thought to play the new record! It's over there somewhere," she gestured vaguely over to the record player before disappearing again and Rosemary had to laugh as she made her way over. It was no secret amongst her friends and family that she was an avid admirer of Frank Sinatra, and Ophelia was always one to indulge her. After a few moments of digging through Ophelia's favorites, Rosemary found Mr. Sinatra's latest release: *Songs for Young Lovers*. There was a moment of crackling, and then the rich voice she loved so much filled the room, and her anxieties instantly calmed.

"Is Mr. Davenport coming tonight?" Rosemary finally asked, walking over to help Ophelia with her row of buttons.

"I invited him, of course." Ophelia's blonde hair, beautifully curled, fell in her face for a moment as she smoothed out the deep blue satin that clung to her. Rosemary helped her with a strand of large pearls, understanding what Ophelia meant. As the newest addition to their summer events, Mr. Davenport's company would be sought after by almost everybody. He must've had dozens of invitations to choose from every evening.

"Someday I'll invite Mr. Sinatra just for you, Rosemary. Wouldn't *that* make for a dinner party?" Ophelia gave herself one more look over before they made their way out of the room and back downstairs.

"It would certainly give me an excuse to have a scotch," Rosemary answered with a laugh, but artfully avoided Ophelia's questioning gaze. No doubt she'd worried her friend, but she didn't have the energy to explain all of her anxieties that evening. Besides, the music had all but washed them away.

"Thomas!" Ophelia's voice was almost too bright as they entered the parlor to see that Mr. Davenport had, in fact, accepted the invitation to dinner that evening. There were a few others as well, whom Rosemary chose to greet instead.

The evening began exactly as every other evening did, fulfilling Rosemary's expectations as well as heavily disappointing them. At least, this was the case until she could no longer avoid Mr. Davenport while still being polite. Rosemary was standing in a corner, drinking her customary glass of sparkling water, and having an incredibly ordinary conversation with Annie Bernard, a small blonde woman with too much money and close-set eyes.

Ophelia had invited her because—unlike many of the others they were forced to interact with during the season—Annie was actually genuinely kind. She was pretty in a simple way, and though not overly fascinating to talk with, she had a calming presence. Rosemary liked her, which was why she felt her anxieties from earlier in the evening all reappear when Annie drifted away somewhere and she saw Mr. Davenport approaching her.

He was wearing a dark suit, embellished with thin, pearl-colored pinstripes. His hair, which had hung a bit in his eyes earlier that day, was now combed off his face. He approached her carrying two glasses of champagne, offering her one silently as he finally reached her side.

"I don't drink, Mr. Davenport," Rosemary said, unclenching her free fist and waving the champagne away politely. "Haven't you heard?" She wondered if his smile was actually brighter now than it had been earlier in the day, or if it was merely a trick of the light.

"I had heard something about that," he responded lightly, setting down the glass he brought for her and taking a sip from his. "I will confess, though, that I didn't entirely believe it and had to see for myself."

"And now that you know?"

"I'm not surprised in the least. Your reputation might precede you, Miss Covington, but it is all favorable." Rosemary cursed herself for not being able to hide her look of surprise well enough, though she covered it by taking a drink of her water. Her reputation hadn't always been that way. But this wasn't something he ever needed to know.

"Did you enjoy boating today?" She asked it to make conversation, because the way his blue eyes stared at her with his eyebrows slightly turned up, as if he were intently searching for something, made her heart pound in a strange way. A not entirely bad way, but certainly not good. She tried to remember her mother's advice, but it was difficult with fear lurking on the edges of her mind. She could think of a thousand things to say that would push him across the room in search of another conversation, but she stopped herself.

"Oh, it was fine. Just fine." He said it in a noncommittal sort of way, draining the last bit of champagne away and looking around for a moment. His eyes settled on two French doors, slightly ajar with a night breeze blowing the curtains. Rosemary knew he was going to ask her to go outside with him, and she couldn't fathom why she found herself agreeing when he did.

They didn't stray far from the house, and for the first several moments, neither of them spoke. Rosemary took several calming breaths of the cool night air, feeling it settle her. What surprised her was that the silence between them wasn't strained. Something about him seemed less electric now that it was just the two of them—it was an almost honest feeling.

"What sorts of hardships have you faced in your life?" Whatever she'd been expecting him to say, it hadn't been that.

"That's a rather personal question, don't you think?" She tilted her head to meet his eyes, now intensely indigo in the dark. The light filtering out from the windows covered half his face, which now held a smile.

"Well, yes," he said with a chuckle, "but how are you supposed to get to know a person if you don't ask those types of questions?"

"I don't see why we need to worry about getting to know one another. I've already told you I would prefer not to be your friend."

"Why is that, Miss Covington?" He stopped walking abruptly, and Rosemary was now violently aware of how close he was standing.

"Because I don't trust you." Even if her insides were tossing about in a mixture of emotions, she kept her voice steady. He looked at her thoughtfully for a moment and then smiled.

"Well, that doesn't surprise me." He turned away from her a bit and pulled a silver case from the inside of his suit, which contained two rows of cigarettes neatly arranged. She watched as he lit one, took a long drag, and then stamped the rest out with the toe of his shoe. They turned together back toward the house, him placing a hand on her elbow as they walked inside. It seemed to burn her skin.

Four

It didn't seem like the ideal time for a business visit. Let alone such an extended one. Mr. Jones stood, rather forlornly, in the huge entryway of a large white house. Holding his hat in one hand and his briefcase in the other, he wondered for perhaps the thousandth time why Miss Baxter would wish the firm to send a representative to her. And for such a long time.

Of course, business trips weren't unheard of, but to come to Newport just as the season of the rich crowd began was another thing entirely. What's more, Miss Baxter had requested his presence for several weeks. She had even found him living accommodations and loaned him the use of one of her cars. She'd fixed everything with the firm weeks ago.

Ophelia Baxter was one of the most prominent clients of a large accounting firm in New York City, of about five or six who stayed in Newport for the season, and the only woman. The branch with which Ophelia did most of her business was known as Harold & Jones, based in Cleveland, Ohio. Besides this basic knowledge, one of the only things Mr. Jones really remembered about Miss Baxter, other than the figures in her accounts, was that because of those figures, Miss Baxter got exactly what she asked for. And this summer, Ophelia had several investments she was in the middle of, as well as a project in Italy that was holding most of her business interest.

With so many things occupying her attention at once, Ophelia saw no reason why the firm couldn't bring business to her, rather than the other way around. They were more than happy to grant her request, as they always were, and once everything was arranged, they sent Mr. Jones off without a second thought. Young though he may be, he was the best in the firm, and Miss Baxter always got the best of everything. And so it was that here he stood, his breath echoing off marble and china.

"Mr. Jones." The young butler who had shown him in before arrived once again, "Miss Baxter is ready for you now. Please follow me." The butler's voice filled the empty space, and as they walked, Mr. Jones had to wonder what the young man was doing as a butler. Despite the color of his skin, Mr. Jones was quite certain he needn't have remained in service. But then again, it wasn't any of his business, and certainly not what he was here to worry about.

The door he was finally led through was tall and white, opening into a beautiful office with a large desk. And behind that was a window overlooking gardens, a strip of silver road, and the ocean. Miss Ophelia Baxter, whom he had only ever heard of with a strange bit of awe, sat behind the desk and smiled brightly when she saw him.

"Hello, Mr. Jones!" She stood and shook his hand firmly, a bit to his surprise, and motioned for him to sit in the cushioned chair across from her.

"It is a pleasure to finally meet you, Miss Baxter," he said, pulling thick files out of his briefcase. "The senior partners at the firm speak very highly of you."

"They have to, don't they?" Mr. Jones was a bit surprised by the comment and more surprised that Miss Baxter then laughed as she put some black-rimmed glasses on the tip of her nose. "You won't be so devastatingly accommodating, will you, Mr. Jones? I'd prefer to work with somebody who isn't afraid to have an opinion. I find far too often that those in the business world are eager to tell me exactly what I want to hear because they understand the value of a bank account, but flattery doesn't make an investment pay."

"Then we'll speak frankly, Miss Baxter." He adjusted his own glasses and pulled out the duplicates of the papers he'd just given her. "You'll be interested to know that your affairs here in the U.S. seem to be in good order. Your oil holdings are just as we projected for the year, as you can see from the charts here. The charts on these pages show your other business interests, which all seem to be more or less as projected. The only investment we're slightly worried about would be your ancestral holdings in the South."

"I understand that Mr. Jones, and as I've told those at the firm, I'm not particularly concerned with gaining any profit there. As long as the plantation can run, I'll keep it."

"I expected as much from reading over the files. I would recommend looking it over, nonetheless. I have some ideas of what could be done to fix the profitability, even if that isn't your main concern."

"I'll read it over tonight and we can discuss it tomorrow," she promised, shuffling through the papers to reach the last file he'd given her. "Let's discuss my Italian project. I trust we were able to secure the property I wanted?"

"Yes, Miss Baxter. There was a bit of trouble in the end, as you requested to buy more of the surrounding property than was originally intended. It required more money, but you did make a contingency fund for that. You'll see it all here."

"I did ask that a representative go and survey the holdings to make sure it was in accordance with my wishes. I'd have gone myself but I was in the middle of other business, as I'm sure you'll remember. I trust that visit went well if I now own the property?"

"Yes, of course. You'll find an extensive report of that here." They continued to discuss business for the better part of the morning until Miss Baxter set her glasses down decisively and began sorting reports and charts back into their proper places.

"I think that is quite enough for today, Mr. Jones. Why don't you join me for lunch and then I'll have you taken to your accommodations." She led him through the house, which seemed even bigger once he began to see more of it, with an energy that seemed impossible for somebody who'd spent an entire morning bending over charts and oil reports. "Oh, and I'll be having a dinner here tonight at seven with just a few friends. You're more than welcome to join us." Aware that he'd somehow slipped into a strange reality, Mr. Jones found himself agreeing.

The accommodations for Mr. Jones turned out to be a guest cottage of Miss Baxter's. It was located not far from the main house, accessible by a thin stone pathway or its own private drive. When Mr. Jones arrived there after his lunch with Miss Baxter—which had consisted of a delicate range of seafood—his things had been dropped off in the main room. He couldn't help but note that what was referred to as a guest "cottage" was closer in size to the large houses of his more affluent friends back home.

He found plenty of food in the kitchen, which was no less than exhilarating, before he explored the rest of the house. It had three bedrooms, a range of rather useless looking parlors, a nice-sized dining room, a music room, and a library. It was the first truly exciting thing he'd found since arriving there, besides all the food in the kitchen, of course. Prying himself away from the shelves, which were unsurprisingly full of treasures, he made his way through unpacking and finally sat down to his work.

The desk was situated directly in front of a window, which seemed to offer him more of a distraction than anything. Instead of looking over the files, he found himself watching a tennis match. It looked like Miss Baxter had joined some of her friends—presumably the ones he'd have to meet that evening. She was playing well, against a woman with auburn hair made fiery red in the sunlight. He could almost imagine what sort of banter they might be sharing or the comments from the cluster of guys standing nearby. Probably something about the style of tennis clothing. He shook his head at the absurdity of it, pretending that he wasn't fascinated.

Five

The only sound Rosemary heard was the soft turning of the record. She'd been home from their tennis match for quite some time now, lying on her bed and wishing she could escape into her music for much longer than she had time for. It always seemed to help on days like this: when her mind was full of things that each needed to be carefully sorted through and put into their proper place. It was rather like a vigorous mental cleaning—and in her experience, best done when there was ample time to do it.

She finally climbed off her bed and wandered over to the record player, replacing the vinyl she'd just finished listening to with *Frankly Sentimental*. It was one of her favorites from Mr. Sinatra, released in '49 and given to her as a birthday gift. She'd listened to it so often that it was nearly worn down now. As *Body and Soul* began to play, Rosemary changed into a silk robe, washed her face, and sat at her vanity table—all with a mechanical sort of movement. There she brushed through her hair for a long while, starting at the roots and moving clear to the end where the waves bounced back up.

The tennis matches had been rather pleasant that afternoon, and certainly more stimulating than lounging on a boat. She always enjoyed a good afternoon of tennis, particularly against Ophelia. They were quite equally matched, and as such, it was always a healthy challenge, though she hadn't had much of an opportunity to play against Ophelia that day. They had only just begun their game when Mr. Davenport trotted over from where he'd been bantering with some of the other guys and somehow managed to wheedle his way into the game. The fact that he'd done that was irritating. Though not nearly as much as the realization that she hadn't really minded. This seemed to be the case with most things that included Thomas Davenport. He seemed to embody everything she disagreed with, and yet she couldn't ever seem to shake him away. It was precisely this that made him dangerous.

Rosemary's door suddenly flew open, and her younger sister, Hazel, came bounding in, blonde hair streaming behind her.

"Can I sit with you while you get ready?" She didn't wait for an answer, but drifted into the closet and began rustling through gowns. "What are you wearing tonight?"

"Why don't you choose for me?" Rosemary replied. Hazel emerged only a second later, holding a gorgeous mustard yellow dress but suddenly stopped.

"What's the matter?"

"Why do you ask?" Rosemary wondered, turning to look in Hazel's concerned eyes.

"You're listening to Frank Sinatra."

"I always listen to Frank Sinatra."

"But this is the record you listen to particularly when you're upset." Just as Hazel said these words, *One for My Baby* began playing. It happened to be Rosemary's favorite on the record. Or perhaps of all of Mr. Sinatra's songs. She could never decide. She took a deep breath, which seemed to be the invitation Hazel was looking for. She set the dress aside and came and sat close to Rosemary, interest and concern mingling on her young face.

"It's Thomas Davenport," Rosemary said all in a rush, suddenly feeling as though saying those three words put her thoughts back in order.

"I've heard some talk about him," Hazel answered with a nod, most likely referring to her afternoon horse rides with some of the other young women she liked to associate with. Rosemary could only imagine what kind of talk went around about him in that particular circle.

"Well, anyway… He's just confusing me, that's all. He's been at most of the events the last week or so, and the way he acts bothers me. Yet I feel drawn to him somehow, which also disgusts me. It brings up some old…memories. Things I'd rather leave in the past." Rosemary had never dared confide in her younger sister this way and yet was astonished when Hazel silently absorbed the information, taking it in with surprising calm.

"Are you in love with him?" Hazel might as well have slapped her.

"No! Of course not! Hazel, I barely know him."

"So you're afraid of him, then," she said in a way that indicated she had convinced herself. "You are remembering painful things and thinking that they are bound to happen again. He reminds you of them, and so he scares you because you haven't come far enough to trust yourself again, let alone anybody else."

Rosemary let out a long breath, silently cursing her younger sister's maturity. Hazel had always had a way of looking at things from a blatant practicality. She was wise beyond her years, and as such seemed to be the pillar of the family. What was more, Rosemary knew that her sister knew nothing of the past hurts she'd acquired aside from occasional references.

"So, what do I do?" Rosemary inquired.

"First, leave your hair down tonight and wear this dress. Second, stop worrying so much, it gives me a headache." Hazel laughed and swept over to the jewelry box as Rosemary began arranging her hair, a smile dancing across her face.

"Mother told me the same thing last week after I met him," Rosemary answered. "And here you are saying it again."

"Well, we have to do that because you're stubborn. We figure that if we say it enough, eventually you'll think it was your idea and you'll listen."

"Oh, good. You're both here." June entered the room then, causing Rosemary to laugh.

She always enjoyed it when they congregated together as mother and daughters. She had many fond memories of just such times.

"Mother, this dress for Rosemary?" Hazel lifted up the gown and swung it about, more to be purposefully dramatic than that she needed confirmation on her own choice.

"Oh, yes. That's perfect," June agreed, joining their small circle. "I came to tell you we received a telegram from your Uncle Louis today."

"How is he?" Rosemary could hardly keep her voice steady. Louis was her mother's brother and had always been very close to them. He'd just recently moved to England and it had been some time since they'd heard anything from him.

"Is he enjoying London?" Hazel set the dress down once more and crowded her mother eagerly, as if it would help her get the news more quickly.

"He's thoroughly enjoying it, though he did make a point to say he missed you all," June answered, helping Rosemary pin one side of her hair up and arranging the rest of the curls around her shoulders. "He also mentioned, Rosemary, that he remembered how much you love it there. He hinted that he'd like to look into finding you a job."

"Could he?" Rosemary's heart lurched in surprise and excitement. She'd always planned on putting her schooling to good use but had only ever dreamed of this.

"He won't look into it unless you're willing, of course, but I'd give it some thought."

"London?" Ophelia's eyebrows raised in surprise as she sipped her gin, artfully ignoring her guests as she and Rosemary had a quick conversation. "What do you think? Will you ask him to look for you?"

"I'm not sure," Rosemary admitted, holding her sparkling water but not drinking a drop.

"It seems so exciting and foreign. London has always been a possibility, but I've never dared to believe it. Almost as though it wouldn't be real. What if I get excited for it only to realize it's a dream?"

"Just because the entire upper crust of our society thinks that you getting a degree was useless doesn't mean you should believe that, too. At least ask your uncle to look into it for you. It isn't the same as accepting an offer. You have nothing to lose." Rosemary's heart was pounding just thinking about it. What if it could happen? Did she dare be that happy? Ophelia sensed her hesitation and smiled, briefly touching her arm. "What could be holding you back?"

"Good evening, ladies," Mr. Davenport suddenly appeared beside them, looking far too polished in a black suit, holding a drink in his hand.

"Oh, hello, Thomas!" Ophelia's voice was bright and welcoming, but a slight edge alerted Rosemary that she was slightly irritated at the interruption. But Rosemary was just grateful her friend had been the one to respond. Her own irritation was much more than a slight edge. He couldn't have missed that they were deep in a discussion to which he hadn't been invited. What made him assume that everybody wanted him in all of their conversations? Or their lives, for that matter?

"How are you this evening, Miss Covington?" He turned to her after a moment of speaking with Ophelia.

"Well, thank you." Try as she might, Rosemary couldn't stop the slightest bit of malice from leaking into her words. "Though I was just about to go chat with some of the other guests, Mr. Davenport. Enjoy your evening." She caught a look of slight disapproval in Ophelia's eye as she walked away—something that seemed to say that she should've controlled her irritation just a bit better. Rosemary sent her an apologetic glance before disappearing into the crowd.

Six

He felt uncomfortable. And completely exhilarated. There seemed to be crowds of people, glasses of champagne everywhere, and too many diamonds and sparkling lights with soft music drifting in from an unknown location. It was like a completely terrifying and utterly wonderful dream. He had no idea who most of these people were, though a nagging in the back of his mind suggested that perhaps he should have. They weren't unfriendly, though it seemed that he couldn't just walk up and make conversation with most of them. Did they have to be formally introduced? Did people still do that?

Mr. Jones had spent most of the afternoon working, but just before it was time to come back to the main house for dinner, his nerves had gone wild. He'd not known what to expect, but at the same time knew exactly what he'd find. He'd felt uneasy about mingling with these people for weeks, and yet his curiosity was nearly unbearable. Their extravagant lifestyle was at once deplorable and fascinating. And after an evening in their presence, he couldn't decide if he loved them or hated them.

He took a glass of champagne and went in search of Miss Baxter. He'd not seen her yet that evening, and so hadn't had a chance to thank her for everything. As far as he could tell, dinner would be starting soon, and he had no intention of sitting next to people he'd not even spoken to.

"Mr. Jones!" She found him first, suddenly materializing from the crowd with a drink in her hand. He shouldn't have been surprised that she held a small dog in the other. He vaguely remembered seeing it that afternoon in her office.

"Good evening, Miss Baxter," he answered, cursing himself for feeling so formal when he wanted to feel more comfortable than he was sure he looked.

"I'm glad you made it," she said, setting the dog on the floor. "I'm sorry if it seems too crowded tonight. It's never possible to know who will show up. I'm sure I haven't spoken to half these people in years, but it makes for a good party."

"I just wanted to thank you for everything, Miss Baxter," he said, feeling as though he couldn't possibly make this encounter any worse. Ever full of surprises, she laughed and motioned for him to follow her.

"You're more than welcome." They didn't go far, just to the other end of the large room where the bar seemed to be the focal point of everything. "But let's not dwell on business anymore—the night is young. As such, drink this," she took the full glass of champagne from his hand and replaced it with scotch, "and call me Ophelia, would you?" There didn't seem to be much point in arguing with her, so he quickly drained the drink and set the glass aside.

"I'm not quite sure how to mingle with everybody here," he admitted.

"Neither does anybody else, trust me," she answered, ordering herself a fresh gin. "But if you're going to be here for most of the season, you might as well enjoy yourself."

"How do you enjoy yourself?" He wanted to know, not realizing until he said it how critical it sounded, but she only laughed.

"If anybody understands the ridiculous flamboyance of our lifestyle, Mr. Jones, it is me. And some of the people here. You'll fit in more easily than you think. Have you met my friend Rosemary Covington yet?" Ophelia gestured over to a young woman in a rich yellow dress, who turned out to be the same one he'd seen her playing tennis with earlier that day. She was talking with another young lady, holding a glass of clear liquid and laughing every so often.

"I have not."

"Well if you're looking for stimulating conversation, try that one. Her honesty might shock you, but she's funny, too." Mr. Jones couldn't help laughing at that.

"Have you known each other long?"

"Ages," Ophelia answered. "Take it from me: The best way to become her friend is to annoy her a little bit at first, but intrigue her as well. Don't try to get under her skin or she'll know, and you won't like the outcome. But if you make it past the surface, you won't find a more loyal friend." She looked around a moment as if pointing at all the glitz surrounding them, "And those can be hard to come by around here. It wouldn't hurt to find some while you're among us."

Rosemary had quickly moved from conversation to conversation after her brief encounter with Mr. Davenport and was relieved that her irritation had quickly fled. She preferred to do all she could to enjoy the evening, and not worry so much as Hazel had advised. She did wish she'd had a moment longer to speak with Ophelia about the London possibility, however, as she felt her friend must be right. What, in fact, could be holding her back from such an amazing opportunity? She could feel her own reluctance palpably, hand in hand with excitement and longing, and yet she could not identify the cause of it.

The conversation she was involved in seemed to dissipate quickly, leaving her with no memory of how it began or what it entailed as she drifted away. She hoped dinner would start soon if only to move the night along. She could almost sense that Thomas Davenport would show up at her side any moment, still holding a drink and flashing his crooked smile. And would she still be angry with him then?

She drifted into another room, hoping to find Ophelia, and instead found herself in the middle of a group of men holding drinks and looking rather important.

"Pandering to them isn't going to change anything." John Blamey said this, an older man who brought his family to Newport from South Carolina every year. His hair was graying at the temples and his accent was a loosely controlled drawl. "They already have the vote. Anything else is crazy." It didn't take much to understand what they were talking about. Rosemary was surprised that this was one of the only conversations she'd stumbled onto about *Brown vs. Board of Education of Topeka*. The controversy of it was heavy everywhere.

"Times are changing everywhere, John." Someone said this over the rim of a bourbon. "It was really only a matter of time."

"Don't bore me with your progressive ideals," Blamey shot back. "Tradition is what lasts. The right way of things."

"And what might that way be, Mr. Blamey?" Rosemary asked, keeping her voice at a level of cool curiosity. He didn't know her well enough to know she was challenging him.

"Oh, Miss Covington." Blamey looked at her with a condescending sweetness, as if he'd just realized she was there. He gestured over to the bar, ordering her a drink. "People form places in society as a natural order of things. They fall into the niches for which they are meant. Altering that is unnecessary and messy. This whole business with the Supreme Court is nothing more than a stunt to satisfy the radicals. Nothing will come of it because nothing ought to." Rosemary pursed her lips and turned to take the sparkling water from the tray that appeared beside her. She looked up into Anthony's dark eyes for the merest second.

"Wouldn't you agree?" It was the merest second before everyone in the circle realized who Blamey was talking to. Anthony looked up from the now empty tray which he then tucked under his arm.

"I believe the decision was unanimous, Mr. Blamey. I also understand that the Supreme Court is charged with interpreting laws and having the final say as to what is and is not lawful according to our constitution. Wouldn't you agree?" The sounds of the party happening around them seemed only like walls to enclose the silence and tension that crept over their circle after Anthony spoke these words.

John Blamey's eyes narrowed dangerously and his grip tightened on his drink.

"Quite." The word was ground out harshly, and in response, Anthony only gave Rosemary a slight bow and walked away. She gave a small smile at his back and left the group with a meaningful glance of her own.

"Rosemary!" She turned then to find her friend gliding into the room, followed by a man Rosemary had never seen before. He wore a well-tailored suit with a bow tie, and his dark hair was combed a bit messily to the side as if he'd meant it to be that way. A pair of dark glasses sat comfortably on his face, along with an unpolished grin. Whoever he was, Rosemary knew instantly he was an outsider. Her curiosity sprung up just at the thought. What in the world would he be doing here, of all places to be?

"Ophelia, who is your new guest?" Rosemary asked politely, her suspicions confirmed when she looked into genuine brown eyes.

"This is Donald Jones. He's been sent here by my accounting firm for most of the season to help me with some of my ventures. I was hoping you could show him the ropes this evening. He's only just arrived today."

"And you're already forcing him to join all of us? God bless you, Mr. Jones." He laughed at that and shook her hand.

"A pleasure to meet you, Miss Covington," he answered. "Ophelia has told me a bit about you."

"She tends to do that," Rosemary answered, getting a laugh from Ophelia and a look that indicated she had not forgotten about what had happened earlier. Ophelia could be infuriating that way, always tugging at issues Rosemary would rather shut away.

"I'm told you have a degree from Radcliffe," Mr. Jones said as they made their way to the dining room, dinner having finally been announced.

"Yes, that's right," Rosemary answered. "I only recently graduated."

"What did you study?"

"Journalism."

"And now what?"

"Survival." Rosemary was suddenly famished and wondered a bit at this young accountant. He seemed a bit uncomfortable amongst all of them, understandably so, but at the same time, he also seemed to strangely belong.

"Where are you from, Mr. Jones?" thinking that perhaps if she asked the questions, the conversation could stay in her control.

"Cleveland, Ohio," he answered, helping himself to a generous portion of mashed potatoes. He seemed unable to contain his excitement that it was finally time to eat, and that brought a genuine smile to Rosemary's lips. Though he did hide it well, she could only imagine how overwhelming this whole experience was for him. Perhaps she'd be excited about something as ordinary as dinner, were she in the same shoes.

"And what's your story?" She asked it to help him feel more comfortable, to help him settle in a bit more. And besides, she was more than a little curious.

"I work for my father's accounting firm, Harold & Jones. I've only been working there for a few years since I finished getting a degree myself."

"Why accounting?"

"Why journalism?" Rosemary had to laugh at that.

"I'm naturally curious, I have a talent for writing, and I enjoy learning. Your turn."

"I enjoy mathematics." Rosemary nearly choked on her food and quickly had to take a drink, which made him laugh. "Which I see you don't."

"Not in the slightest. But we all have our areas of expertise." She took a sip of water and turned to him thoughtfully. "Did you always want to follow your father into accounting? Was there ever anything else you dreamed of being or doing?" She was surprised at how the look in his eyes changed from one of soft enjoyment to one of depth as if several layers had been peeled back at once before they were ready.

In any other situation, she may have just come out and asked him what he was thinking, if not for that fact that she'd felt that exact same way only earlier that day. For the first time in the longest time, Rosemary realized that she wasn't the only one who seemed to be navigating dangerous waters, simultaneously fearing and needing the shore. She looked down the table and saw Mr. Davenport's eyes find hers. He smiled.

Later that night, or really closer to the morning, when the after-dinner cocktails had long since been put away, Rosemary made her way to the front parlor of Ophelia's house. She'd phoned home to say that one of Ophelia's drivers would bring her back, somehow knowing she would be staying unnaturally late that evening. She'd spent a good portion of the evening talking with Donald Jones before he'd been clever enough to retire early. It had proven to be one of the most stimulating conversations she'd ever experienced.

Rosemary was impressed with how he'd managed to blend in with everybody so quickly, making conversation with many people at the table. It was clear to her why he was doing so well in his chosen field, even if he seemed incredibly young to be the one out with large clients. He was a natural around all different kinds of people and somehow had the ability to merge seamlessly with those around him. She envied him that skill.

She'd stayed later than usual that evening because she knew Ophelia wanted to speak with her and to be honest, she wanted to speak with Ophelia. If there was anybody who could help her sort out her anxieties as far as the London possibility was concerned, it was Ophelia Baxter. But waiting to speak with her meant that Rosemary had to stay longer than anybody else. And that night the guests were particularly chatty.

Rosemary finally arrived at the parlor, where she was sure Ophelia would've been bidding farewell to guests and talking with others. She did find her there, but deep in conversation with Anthony. Ophelia saw Rosemary from the corner of her eye and indicated that she should wait, quickly finishing her conversation and walking wearily over to her friend, as if she hadn't allowed herself to feel tired until that moment.

"I'm getting much too old for this," Ophelia joked, glancing at the clock which indicated it was 4:30 am. Rosemary nodded and held in a yawn. "I know we need to talk some more about London, Rosemary, but let's wait until tomorrow. I promise I haven't forgotten."

"I agree," Rosemary answered sleepily, accepting Ophelia's hug gratefully and letting her lead the way to the front door. "It was a lovely evening, Ophelia. They'll be talking about this all season."

"That's what I was hoping for," Rosemary laughed and hugged Ophelia one more time before leaving the glowing white house behind her. She took a deep breath of the early morning air, somehow feeling in it that in only a few hours, the sun would rise. But for now, the stars still glowed brightly, tiny specks of light glinting at her.

"Miss Covington?" The voice was soft and somewhat hesitant. She turned to see Thomas Davenport sitting on the marble steps. His suit was still perfectly pressed, but his usually sleek hair was mussed and his tie loose. He held his hat in his hands as if he'd been shuffling it nervously between them. Her fingers flinched instinctively, ready to clench into fists for her irritatingly punctual nervous habit.

"Yes?" She was suddenly too tired to muster up any of her previous irritation, even when she knew perfectly well how foolish the whole fiasco had been. Her mind had settled into the logical point beyond tired—when the thoughts come together in conclusions they wouldn't have had the chance to otherwise. It had been far too long of a night for her to put energy into not trusting him. For reasons she couldn't explain, she suddenly no longer felt the need to push away the magnetic field that surrounded him.

He stood and approached her somewhat nervously, and Rosemary had the thought that perhaps neither of them were quite themselves this early in the morning after such an evening.

But maybe that was a good thing. With all the pretense and banter stripped away, they were only two people leaving a party.

"Could I, that is, would you allow me to drive you home?" She found herself smiling and nodding, too tired to argue as he escorted her a ways down the drive to his car. It was the very latest Corvette, and as brilliantly blue as his eyes. It had just two seats, no top, and thick whitewall tires. She sank into the leather seat gratefully when he opened the door for her, and his shoes made crunching noises on the gravel as he moved around to the driver's side.

They didn't say anything on the short drive to her house, but the silence wasn't strained. Rosemary leaned her head back and let the breeze run through her hair, nearly laughing at how refreshing it felt. He pulled the car slowly up the drive and shifted into park, though he didn't shut it off as he walked around and escorted her up the steps to the door.

"Rosemary?" She looked into his eyes, shocked to see that they seemed completely clear—as if she could look into their very center. It was the most genuine she'd ever seen him.

"Yes?"

"I wanted to apologize for earlier this evening. For anything I've done that might have offended you."

"Don't think anything of it," she answered. "Thank you for driving me home."

"You're very welcome." He flashed her his crooked smile before making his way down the steps toward his car, though after a few steps, he turned back to look at her. "Can we please be friends?"

She only hesitated one moment before shaking her head with a smile and realized that there was really only one word that could be used to describe this man: inevitable.

"I think that would be just fine, Thomas." His smile broadened as she entered the house and closed the door softly behind her, not wanting to wake anybody. She turned to peek out of a window, watching as he quickly lit a cigarette and took one long breath before tossing it away. She could still see his smile as he drove out of sight.

Seven

Several days later was the first big charity ball of the season, to be held at the Pools' mansion which, though very large, would surely be bursting at the seams with jewels and cigarettes. Rosemary rode over to the ball with her parents in a sleek black Rolls-Royce with windows so clean that they looked invisible. Her mother looked stunning in a burgundy colored gown with her blonde hair swept up high on her head, and her father looked immensely proud in his flawless tuxedo.

Arthur Covington was at best distracted and at worst indifferent, but beneath it all, he was a good man. This was able to shine through when he looked at his wife in admiration as they drove on in silence. Rosemary turned her head away and looked out of the window, feeling nervous for reasons she didn't know. She hadn't seen Thomas since he'd driven her home some nights before, and since then, she'd finally had that talk with Ophelia. It had consisted of many things, most of which Rosemary had predicted: Ophelia urging her to have more faith in humanity, to see Thomas as an opportunity to learn how to trust again, and let Uncle Louis look into a job for her in London.

Rosemary wanted to be open-minded about it, mostly because she knew Ophelia was often right and wiser than Rosemary could ever hope to be. But her stubbornness welled inside of her and she was tempted to do the exact opposite of all her friend had said just for the sake of doing it. This kind of blatant rebellion was a red hot streak in Rosemary's personality, one that had often given her trouble. The paradox of it was that she knew it was a weakness she could easily overcome, but she often disregarded this thought just to be rebellious.

"You look lovely tonight, my dear," June told her just before they arrived, and Rosemary gladly accepted the compliment along with the loving look from her mother. It helped soothe her fears, though part of her still wished she could be at home with Hazel. Sometimes she missed the days of being just young enough that she couldn't attend these parties.

The mansion was lit from foundation to roof, glowing with a yellow light that seemed to be all at once stuck in the house and bursting from it. The moment they stepped into the door, flashing a shimmering invitation, music filled their ears and Rosemary felt as though they were carried into the heart of the party on a cloud of music and champagne.

"Rosemary!" Ophelia approached her from the crowd, a drink in her hand and a smile brilliant on her face as she surveyed the gown Rosemary wore. "How very Grace Kelly."

That evening, Ophelia wore a form-fitting black gown with a deep neck, embellished with a gorgeous strand of heavy pearls. Her hair was curled and combed back from her face, and her lips were a soft pink. She was absolutely the picture of elegance, and more than half of the men present seemed to notice. But she simply laughed and shook her head, steering Rosemary away from prying eyes and twirling couples toward the back of the ballroom.

"Nonsense, you're much more Grace Kelly than I'll ever be," Rosemary answered, gladly taking a glass of sparkling water a waiter brought her. She was grateful somebody had thought to send it over to her, probably her parents.

"Have you given any more thought to London?" Ophelia asked, setting her drink aside to light a cigarette, perching the holder in her right hand.

"A bit," Rosemary admitted, "though not much. I've been a little distracted." Ophelia didn't have to ask what she meant, particularly because they saw the answer approaching them through the crowd, wearing a white tuxedo jacket on his broad shoulders and a brilliant smile. Rosemary briefly wondered how vibrant his eyes would be that night. It always seemed to change.

"I've come to ask for the pleasure of a dance, Ophelia," Thomas said, giving Ophelia his most award-winning smile and getting a laugh from it.

"I'd love to, Thomas," she answered, putting out the rest of her cigarette and letting him lead her out onto the dance floor. Rosemary had to laugh at it all, sipping at her water and swaying softly to the music, her full skirt swishing. She often got the impression that Ophelia didn't exactly know what to make of Thomas, but decided to enjoy his company regardless. She had a way of doing that with just about anybody, in fact. Rosemary could hear their laughter even as they glided skillfully across the room.

She was surprised a few moments later when she saw Donald Jones appearing from the crowd, looking like he'd been born there rather than forced in only days before. She hadn't expected him to be there that evening, though she had to smile at the way he seemed to naturally blend in with those around him, and only wondered briefly if somebody like that had anything that was constant about them.

"Hello, Miss Covington," he said as he approached her, smiling so genuinely that his dark eyes became slits. There was something about him that felt very open and inviting, something warm and familiar. Perhaps that was why he fit in so well.

"Hello, Mr. Jones," Rosemary answered, glimpsing Thomas and Ophelia through the crowd and feeling her heart lift. "I didn't expect to see you here tonight."

"I tried valiantly if that means anything, but Ophelia insisted that I come," he replied, taking a glass of champagne from a nearby waiter.

"You seem to be enjoying yourself, though. How do you make so many friends wherever you go?" It seemed as though he could be warm and genuine in the most sincere way, and yet there was something hesitant in him. But it was a very subtle hesitance, as though he couldn't quite decide what to make of everything around him and had stowed the thoughts away for later.

The very idea intrigued her for the simple reason that she often did the same thing.

"People interest me," he answered with a shrug. "What about you, Miss Covington? What interests you?"

"Ideas," she answered immediately. "Literature. History. People do in a way, I suppose, but more the stories that hide behind them. Everybody here has a story, Mr. Jones, behind the taffeta and diamonds."

"How do you find those stories out?"

"By listening," Rosemary answered, finishing her water and folding her arms lightly across her chest, "and watching. People reveal far more just by being than they realize. Some stories aren't meant to be found out, but it only adds to the mystery of it all."

"You left out philosophy on the list of things you enjoy." Rosemary realized he was teasing her and they laughed a bit. "But I do understand what you mean. You're one of the brave ones who aren't afraid to get lost in their mind. In thoughts like that."

"I think we all do, in some way or another," she answered, and was surprised when he nodded as if he truly understood. She'd never know what he might have been about to say, however, as Ophelia and Thomas's dance had ended and before she knew it, she'd been swept up in a dance herself.

"You look beautiful tonight, Rosemary." Thomas said it in a very natural way as if it weren't a compliment but a remark on the weather. She wished it hadn't made her blush.

"You don't usually wear bow ties," she commented, moving her hand from his shoulder to straighten the black tie. It hadn't been extremely crooked, but it was something to look at besides his eyes. They were so blue tonight that it almost hurt.

"I thought I'd try and blend in with the crowd," he answered with his crooked smile, which made her laugh and shake her head.

"Blending into the crowd isn't something you'll ever do, Thomas. I'm not sure you know how."

"Whereas you seem to avoid being noticed at all costs." Rosemary was vaguely aware of the song changing as he said this, but they simply kept dancing. "Why is that?"

"I prefer to observe others instead of being noticed by them. If I have to be noticed by others, it is something I can live with, but it isn't my choice. Honestly, I think that I just think too much." Thomas laughed at that and nodded as if he agreed.

"Do you ever get tired of thinking your way through life?" If he'd asked her this question a week or so before, it might have made her angry. But now she felt it sink into her heart, understanding just how correct he was. She did think her way through life, she did prefer to stand on the fringes rather than be engaged in living. The true reasons why she preferred it weren't ones he even knew about. But still, he'd managed to see it anyway.

"Yes." It was a simple answer, but Thomas seemed to understand just how much it contained. He was silent for a moment as they continued their dance, and eventually, he led her off the dance floor and into one of the adjoining rooms. Though it seemed that no matter where they went, the rooms were full of people, and so they finally exited the house into the fresh summer night.

"Where are we going?" she asked, her free hand clenched into a fist—as if she held all her nerves inside of it. But she knew she was feeling nervous only because he was the one leading the way. He turned and met her eyes, surprising her with his smile. It looked as though he was full of some sort of happiness, as if he hadn't been able to stand being in the party and could now glory in being liberated from it.

"Rosemary, do you trust me?" Every initial fear sprung up into her throat and choked her for a moment, begging her to say no—to run back into the party where she would be uncomfortable for the rest of the night. But Ophelia would be inside, and suddenly Rosemary remembered what her friend had told her only days before. Perhaps Thomas was an opportunity.

And suddenly Rosemary couldn't stop smiling, almost to the point where she laughed.

"Yes, I do."

Hand in hand, they ran away from the party. Rosemary's taffeta skirt blew behind them, and pins from her hair came loose. Thomas surprised her by pulling off his bow tie and throwing it as they ran around the side of the house and toward the drive where his car waited for them.

Rosemary held her high heels in one hand and Thomas's hand in the other, feeling a liberation she couldn't remember if she'd ever felt. When they arrived at his car, she tossed her shoes inside and climbed in over the door, making him laugh as he ran to his side and jumped in.

The rest of Rosemary's hair came tumbling down as they zoomed away, the car throwing gravel out behind it as the overflowing house dissolved into its own retreating light. She pulled her feet up next to her on the leather seat and put her hands in the air, laughing as Thomas drove faster and faster. She wasn't sure if she would regret feeling this way tomorrow, or if she'd be angry for allowing herself to feel this kind of wild happiness. But she decided to wait and find out in the morning rather than dwell on it then.

"Where are you taking me?" She could barely say it over her laughter.

"Anywhere but that party," he laughed with her and drove just a bit faster. It felt like they drove for hours and yet not long enough, but eventually, Thomas pulled his car up at the dock and jumped out. Rosemary followed close behind him, and he held her hand tightly as they ran past the rows of peacefully bobbing boats. Looking back, Rosemary would never remember if they had been the only ones driving on the road or at the dock that night. She'd been far too busy ignoring her fears to notice.

He brought her to two boats that were his and jumped past the regular yacht into the speedboat. It was a beautiful boat, with dark wood paneling that gleamed in the moonlight and two rows of white leather seats. Once he was securely inside, he grabbed her by the waist and lifted her inside with him, grinning as they settled back into the seats and once again sped away.

Rosemary had been boating at night before—several times, in fact. But she didn't think that the moon had ever been quite this bright. It was almost like the sun. It cast the shadow of their smiles on the white seats and illuminated the foam that sprayed out behind the boat. Thomas held the steering wheel firmly with one hand, expertly maneuvering the boat as if he'd been driving it as long as he'd drawn breath, and held her hand securely with his free hand.

The roar of the boat was too loud for them to have any sort of normal conversation at first, but perhaps that was the point of the evening. She didn't know if she really wanted to talk anymore about what they had been discussing earlier. She felt utterly fearless and exhilarated, and couldn't remember the last time she'd experienced either of those things.

After a moment, Thomas slowed the boat down, turning back toward Newport where they could see lights glittering back at them. Endless amounts of boats dotted the water with sleek white sails reflecting the moonlight. They nodded in the greeting of the waves and waited for the next outing. Thomas eventually slowed the boat, not seeming to mind floating wherever the water might pull them.

The air was chilly out on the water, with the breeze blowing across it and onto them.

Thomas let go of her hand just long enough to slip out of his white suit coat and drape it over her shoulders. He took a moment to gently pull her hair out from underneath the collar, and she realized her cheeks were beginning to hurt from so much smiling.

"Will you still be this happy in the morning?" His voice was incredibly soft as he said it, almost timid.

"I hope so." She looked into his eyes for one moment that seemed to electrify her very soul, and then he kissed her.

Eight

That first time Thomas Davenport kissed her, Rosemary felt a relief so deep that it was shocking. It was relief for many things, but mostly because she felt as though everything she'd been holding back finally let go. She made a decision at that moment to not think about her fears, to not think about the things that had happened to her, and certainly not think about the future. She would only think about each moment.

She didn't realize until then how long it had been since she'd allowed herself to truly live, and how beautiful the experience could be. Thomas frightened her in many ways, mostly because he made her feel everything she'd always sworn she'd never feel again. But perhaps that was the point. From the first moment she'd met him, Rosemary had known Thomas was the kind of person who could see that she hid things.

It wasn't a long kiss, and overall it was rather timid. In the seconds that followed, as Rosemary's heart pounded and Thomas pulled his hands away from her face, it felt as though a great crossroads stretched out before her. But yet she knew it had stretched before her long ago, and despite how careful she'd wanted to be, she had already made her decision. She let out a shaky breath and sat back for only a moment before nestling into his open arms, her head resting against his steadily beating heart. And for a long time, they didn't move or speak, but only watched the glittering lights winking at them from shore.

Eventually, Thomas guided the boat to the dock and secured it. But they didn't leave. They settled into the seats, covered in a light blanket Thomas had found in the back, and talked until most of the twinkling lights went out. When Rosemary thought on it later, she realized that in general, they didn't talk about anything important, nothing specific or heart-opening.

Rosemary did tell him a bit about her journalism and how she wanted to eventually use her degree. He told her about his divorced parents. But then the talk moved into Rosemary's favorite books and Thomas's love of baseball. He let her go on and on about Frank Sinatra, and laughed and agreed with most of what she said.

At some point, the talk must have dwindled, or perhaps they fell asleep at the same time. But the next thing Rosemary was aware of was peach-colored light and crisp morning air. Thomas's arm was heavy around her, and his chest still rose and fell in the deep breathing of sleep. She let herself wake up a bit, rubbing the corners of her eyes and pushing her curls behind her ear.

She sat very still, not wanting to wake him yet, and waited for her senses to catch up with her. She waited for a wave of guilt, panic, heart-crushing fear, or the urge to run. But none of those things came. There were only memories of one kiss and hours of conversation. Upon realizing this,

Rosemary decided to wake Thomas up before her feelings changed their mind.

It didn't take long for his eyes to open once she wiggled out from under his arm, and she couldn't help but smile as he sat up and revealed his mussed hair. He chuckled a bit at realizing she was teasing him and rubbed his eyes.

"Good morning, Rosemary." His voice was scratchy with sleep.

"Good morning, Thomas." She pulled the blanket off them and arranged her now very crumpled skirt before reaching up to smooth out his rather remarkable hairdo, which made her laugh. After a moment, he stood and jumped onto the dock, his dress shirt now mostly untucked and his pants hopelessly wrinkled. As he reached back to help her from the boat, she noticed a boyish innocence clinging to him that she'd have never predicted he possessed. But then again, everything looked perfect this morning.

They walked hand in hand back down the dock, Rosemary still wearing his suit coat with her bare feet peeking out from under her dress. There was a feeling of quiet peace surrounding them as they approached the car— as if the world was pausing for breath just before it woke up.

The Covington mansion was still dark inside when they arrived, as if unwilling to leave the lingering magic of the night before. Thomas turned the car off before he walked Rosemary to the door. There was a small moment of silence when Rosemary wasn't sure what would happen next.

"When can I see you again?" It was at that moment that Rosemary realized Thomas had been afraid. Afraid that all of her feelings would catch up with her that morning. He'd been afraid she would run. And she couldn't blame him.

"Whenever you like," she answered, and she received a smile in return that was so brilliant that it could've dazzled the strongest of hearts. He looked down at their intertwined hands for a moment before leaning forward to press a kiss to her cheek. She watched him drive away before entering the house and quietly making her way to her room, still wearing his suit coat.

The life of Ophelia Baxter would have made a spectacular movie. It was something that Rosemary had thought often, though she could never quite decide which actress would be perfect to play Ophelia. Deborah Kerr would be magnificent at showing Ophelia's business sense and presence of mind, yet Marilyn Monroe would certainly show the side of Ophelia that was, for all her wealth and business, still a young woman in her prime. Grace Kelly was almost too perfect for the role, but then again, Rosemary had always viewed the sensational actress as much too good for the world at large.

Rosemary was lost in these thoughts later that day as she drove to Ophelia's in the most recent gift from her father: a 1954 Jaguar. It was a deep pine green with wide whitewall tires and smooth leather seats, and most of all, Rosemary thought it was far too much. But she had learned long ago that when it came to gifts from her father, it was best to accept them with complete gratitude and leave it at that. Arthur Covington took great pride in caring for his daughters. Though his version of caring for them was much more expensive than Rosemary thought it needed to be. But such was the life of the Newport crowd.

Rosemary parked the car on Ophelia's drive and sprung up the stairs toward the door, her white ballet flats making happy tapping noises that betrayed all her secrets. She was surprised when somebody other than Anthony answered the door, but was shown quickly to the back patio where Ophelia was already enjoying the sun and some iced tea.

"Good afternoon!" she said, settling onto a cushioned chair. "Where is Anthony today?"

"Good afternoon to you as well," Ophelia said, her face a mix of sly understanding and laughter. "Today is Anthony's day off; he gets a few every month and this time, he took them all at once. Probably escaping the season."

"How do you manage without him here?" Rosemary teased, taking a glass of tea.

"I'm honestly not sure," Ophelia answered with a laugh, "I always think I'll manage fine without him, and then he goes. That's when I'm forced to confront how well he keeps everything put together."

Rosemary nodded her understanding as she took a sip of her drink, looking past the guest cottage occupied by Mr. Jones and toward the ocean. Everything seemed a little bit more brilliant in color that day, from the navy blue of her pressed trousers to the green of the grass. Ophelia's hair looked more golden than usual. Even Ralph, nestled next to Ophelia in the cushions, looked different.

"What are you thinking about?" her friend asked, her voice more than prodding.

"I was thinking about how your life would make a fantastic movie," Rosemary answered, meeting Ophelia's eyes eagerly. "I've been thinking about it the whole drive over here. The only thing your life really lacks is some great secret to make things exceptionally thrilling."

"Speaking of secrets," Ophelia said, expertly moving the conversation away from Rosemary's attempted dodge, "you are keeping one yourself. Tell me absolutely everything or suffer the consequences."

"I'm afraid that if you're looking for a juicy scandal, you'll be disappointed," Rosemary laughed. "First, you have to tell me everything everybody said after we left the party."

"Most everybody was too drunk by then to notice," Ophelia commented, waving a hand in dismissal, "which makes me sure that your evening was much more happily spent than mine. You weren't horrible to him, were you?"

"Not overly, anyway," Rosemary said with a laugh, drinking some more of her tea before finally telling her friend *mostly* everything. There were some moments that now seemed too sweet to share.

"And you didn't get in until early this morning!" Ophelia finally said, leaning back in her chair with wide eyes and the shadow of a smile. "So what are you thinking about it?"

"I'm not entirely sure, but to be honest, I'd like to keep it that way. The moment I think about it deeply enough to have an opinion, I'm afraid I'll run, and I'm thoroughly enjoying just being happy." Her friend nodded in understanding but continued to sit back in her chair with her legs crossed, petting Ralph absently as if she couldn't really believe everything that had happened. It seemed that the feeling was mutual amongst all involved.

"How are things going with Mr. Jones?" Rosemary asked sometime later, finishing her iced tea as she looked over at the guest cottage. It looked strangely empty for having an occupant.

"Very well," Ophelia answered, scooping the dog into her arms and leading the way back inside. "He's very good at what he does, clearly, which I'm grateful for. He's been invaluable in some projects I'm doing in Europe this year. The only concern I have is that he really doesn't seem to be enjoying himself, which seems petty considering the fact that he is here to do business after all."

"What makes you say that?" Rosemary wondered, making her way over to Ophelia's records once they entered her room.

"He spends most of his free time in town, which is good, though what he does there is beyond me. I'm glad he's taking advantage of the car, at least."

"Do you suppose he's unimpressed with the rich crowd?" she said teasingly, though sensed it was perhaps more correct than either she or Ophelia knew. She got the feeling that Mr. Jones enjoyed being in Newport the way one enjoyed being at a fair: it was nice for the show, just to see what happened, but at some point, one needed a break to enjoy what was real in the world.

"In some ways, yes," Ophelia answered emphatically. "And yet, I get the impression that we intrigue him. It's almost as if he knows he'll get sucked inside the ridiculousness of it all, but he does it anyway."

"How fascinating," Rosemary commented lightly as she put a record on. "Maybe I'll interview him. See what's going on inside that head of his."

"Well I wish you'd do something," her friend answered, her voice now coming from deep inside the closet. "If you remember, I volunteered you to be his friend while he's here and you've done a terrible job. Though I will admit it may not be entirely your fault. Maybe I'll complain to Thomas."

"I wish you'd make up your mind about who I'm supposed to be spending my time with," Rosemary bantered back, helping her bring out a stack of dresses she was sending back to the designers. Ophelia was incredibly picky when it came to clothing, and rarely kept anything she was sent. But Rosemary happened to know that it was because Ophelia avoided spending money unnecessarily.

"The jazz festival is coming up," Ophelia commented some moments later through the soft turning of music and rustle of fabric. "Are you still planning to go?"

"Of course!" Rosemary answered. "I'm very excited about it, actually. You know that there will be lectures as well as live performances?"

"Well, it wasn't too long ago that you were thinking you might not attend. I believe it had something to do with the predictability and uselessness of our type of life." Ophelia's eyes danced teasingly, "What was it exactly that changed your mind?"

"Billie Holiday will be performing. It is practically a requirement to attend, especially for somebody with my musical taste." It wasn't exactly untrue, Rosemary had always planned on attending for these very reasons and others. It was the first show of its kind, thought up by the Lorillards, who were family friends. But this wasn't what Ophelia was focusing on, not with that knowing smile breaking out across her face. The truth was that many things had been bothering Rosemary earlier in the summer, and suddenly, she couldn't remember what any of them were. A shy happiness was daring to peak through the cracks inside of her. And it was too distracting for her to spend time on anything else. Ophelia knew that as well, which was why she didn't press further.

"I'm glad to see you this happy, Rosemary," Ophelia finally said, and even Grace Kelly couldn't have said it better.

Nine

Donald Jones had long since given up being bored, though the first few days in Newport had nearly driven him crazy. The mornings were always full of the work he'd actually come to do, and he couldn't help but be more and more impressed with Ophelia as things continued. She was a shrewd businesswoman if nothing else.

The evenings were usually taken by some social function he was somehow required to attend, but that always left a long and empty afternoon before him. And there was only so much work one could do. He'd taken to using the library in his temporary home and had read more books since arriving than he had in years. Newport itself had distractions of its own. Many afternoons, he took the car provided for him and spent the day within the city.

Overall, he knew he certainly couldn't complain about his current situation, but it also wasn't something he could easily make sense of. He had never been more immersed in society and still far away from it in his life. Living with these people had a way of tilting his thoughts in strange directions. Such things were often hard for him to make sense of on his own. He had a strange tendency to never be able to quite figure out how something made him feel. And this was no exception.

Newport was an alluring fairytale: a giant scape of jewels and lights, with a dangerous sort of magic. It was all at once too real and painfully artificial. He'd never met people with more presence of mind, with more of an idea of what it meant to live.

But he'd also never been surrounded by more mystery. He'd been living amongst them for long enough now to know that everybody here had secrets. Dark secrets. There was a deeper current running under Newport, and Donald Jones was the only one who could really see it. He just had to wonder when it would all come to a head, as such things inevitably did.

"Deep thoughts this morning, Mr. Jones?" It was Anthony, Ophelia's butler, who asked it as he brought in a tray tinkling with white cups full of coffee. This was usually how the morning began: with him sitting in Ophelia's office for a few moments while he waited for her, his thoughts occupied with other things while Anthony brought in the coffee. He was a very friendly man, and Donald was more than a little fascinated by what his life must be like. But he thought that perhaps it wasn't the sort of thing one asked.

"Yes." The word sounded a little hollow to him, but he managed to give Anthony a grateful smile.

"You'll get used to the Newport life, sir," Anthony surprised him by saying. "But of course, then you'll have to leave again."

"Don't scare the man off, Anthony," Ophelia reprimanded lightly, having walked into the room just then. Anthony bowed his head a bit as if pretending to be chastised, but his bright smile said he wasn't taking her seriously. She rolled her eyes a bit playfully at that as he left the room.

"Good morning, Ophelia," Donald said, never ceasing to be amazed at the energy she always had as she came bouncing into her chair and pulled her coffee over to her. She took it black.

"To you as well, Donald," she answered, tossing him a smile as she pulled out the files they were working through. "Did I overhear that you're not enjoying your stay?"

"On the contrary, Newport is extremely entertaining." He busied himself with getting out his papers.

"A bit too entertaining, it seems," she commented wryly, clearly too observant to be fooled. "I did assign Rosemary to be your friend, and here she is, obviously failing."

"Miss Covington has her mind on other things, I'm sure."

"Indeed." She offered no further explanation, and the rest of the morning seemed to fall away in a flurry of business.

Donald wandered back over to the guest house sometime later, his head full of figures. He felt a strange emptiness that day, a feeling he couldn't exactly name, but he rather suddenly decided to ignore it, as was a habit of his with things he couldn't make sense of—though he reasoned that he was only in Newport for a short time, and only to do business. It wasn't worth all the trouble of getting emotionally involved.

"You cannot seriously be intending to drink this before noon," Rosemary said to Thomas, pulling a bottle of whiskey out of the cooler.

"Not the entire thing, anyway." His voice was teasing as he reached past her and grabbed something else from the cooler, which he then revealed to be a can of peaches. "Sinful as it may be to drink before noon, this is my favorite breakfast." Rosemary watched him open the can, only slightly amused until he opened the whiskey and poured just a bit of it into the can, and then she laughed.

"Thank you for thinking of me, too," she replied, pulling out a raspberry pastry and settling next to him on the deck. He smiled in response, half of a peach on the end of his fork. He'd telephoned her the evening before to ask if she felt like a day of yachting, and now they sat on the back of the boat, looking toward Newport. It wasn't a large yacht, easily managed by the two of them, but that didn't stop it from being beautiful. And most likely very expensive.

Rosemary kicked off her sandals and crossed her feet at the ankles, arranging her floral skirt that unclipped to reveal her bathing suit. It was a style Hazel was wild over, and it made Rosemary smile to think of her younger sister. She'd been practically gushing that morning just before Thomas had come to pick her up, though slightly disappointed that Rosemary didn't have more than three possible bathing suit and skirt options.

"It's a dress and a bathing suit, Rosemary. How did you only pick three with the ocean out the front door?" Hazel had said it as though she wasn't perfectly aware of both facts, and the thought made her laugh.

"What's so funny?" Thomas asked.

"My younger sister Hazel," Rosemary answered. "Sometimes I think we were born in the wrong order."

Thomas nodded thoughtfully, and for a moment, a strange look came into his eyes. "I think it would be nice to have siblings," he finally said, finishing the last peach and then draining the juice and whiskey mixture straight from the can.

"It is," she said, "if for no other reason than that they lecture you on your clothing choices." Thomas laughed then, the light returning to his eyes and making them a shocking blue. To her surprise, he set the now empty can aside and reached over to where her bag lay. It was full of things for the day: towels, sunscreen, and the like. But what he had noticed was the edge of a book peeking out of it, and he laughed as he slid it out of the bag and turned it over in his hands.

"You brought a book boating?" His voice was distinctly teasing, but for some reason, his question made her nervous. As if she suddenly had to explain herself.

"Boating is actually the ideal place to read," she answered. "It is peaceful and nobody bothers you."

"*The Great Gatsby*," Thomas read the cover. "One of your favorites?"

"Most definitely," Rosemary answered, feeling a passion rise inside of her. "It is absolutely incredible. Fitzgerald has such a way with words. Somehow he knows how to address so many human conditions very simply." Thomas nodded as though he understood what she was saying, or at least to the point where he understood why she adored it so much. He smiled then, and before she knew it, he had jumped up and leaped into the water.

They spent most of the day swimming. After a brief lunch pulled from the bottomless cooler, Thomas surprised Rosemary by stretching out on his towel and falling fast asleep. She found that she didn't entirely mind, though. It gave her a chance to read. She made a mental note of several witty things to say in response to Thomas when he awoke, as he would inevitably tease her about it.

All of that quickly melted away in the face of Fitzgerald's words, however, and before she knew it, she was deep within the novel. It didn't matter how many times she'd read it. The story never ceased to take her breath away with its raw beauty.

"I looked that love-struck the first time my dad took me to a baseball game." Thomas's voice was a little sleepy, but thick with a smile. Rosemary peeled her eyes away from the page, not realizing how long it had been and taking a few seconds to sweep her mind clear.

"I'm sure you did. How was your nap?"

"Very refreshing." He jumped up then, as if he hadn't been fast asleep moments earlier, and sauntered over to the cooler. "Water?" Rosemary nodded at his offer, taking the water he handed her and putting her book away somewhat reluctantly. He then took a quick swig of whiskey before gulping down some water himself. It seemed he'd never quit surprising her.

"How is Fitzgerald treating you?"

"Quite well, as always." Thomas flopped down next to her as she answered, somewhat lazily. "Did you have any dreams?"

"I never dream." His tone was nonchalant.

"How sad." Rosemary's voice was teasing as she took another sip of her water, and it made him chuckle. She turned to look directly into his eyes and found that they were slightly veiled. "What are you thinking about?"

"That I would like to kiss you." His honesty was only a little shocking, but his words caused a distantly familiar prickling on the back of her neck. Was it fear? She couldn't remember and didn't have enough time to think about it before she found herself leaning closer to accept his kiss. Her fists clenched as she pushed her arms around his back.

He tasted like sunshine. And whiskey. It was this that compelled her to accept a second and third kiss, each one longer and more intoxicating than the last. Thomas put his hand on her cheek then, pulling her closer. And even then, she couldn't place the feeling. It was only when he momentarily pulled away – just for long enough to sit up a bit and pull her against him – and it disappointed her that she realized what the feeling was. Excitement.

And with that realization came only an ice-cold wave of fear and disgust, and she found herself jerking away abruptly. Chills of fright were running up and down her arms, but she couldn't explain them. Indeed, she couldn't even meet his startled eyes as she quickly stood and jumped into the water.

Ten

There wasn't as much tension between them for the rest of the day as Rosemary had expected. Thomas had a strange softness about him, almost as though he understood what had happened without her having to say it. She wasn't entirely sure that was the case. Thomas happened to be very good at making it seem as though he knew what another person was feeling. But it was comforting, for at least a little while, to entertain the idea that he might.

He didn't take her hand as they walked back to his car from the boat. She supposed that was probably for the best. He did give her several smiles, though, as if to try and reassure her. Rosemary wasn't convinced. Perhaps he felt as though her reaction earlier was something easily explained away, but it wasn't. Especially not when her feelings regarding him were still so timid and unsure.

She'd known since leaving the party with him that night that there would be no turning back. But knowing that and understanding what it meant were two completely different things. The conflict left her feeling oddly jumbled inside. She wished that was a feeling his electric blue eyes could smile away, but it wasn't.

He drove rather slowly back to her home, which she didn't mind. The light was beginning to turn the medieval orange of the afternoon, and the warm breeze traveled through her salt-encrusted hair in an oddly comforting way. With Doris Day, Kitty Kallen, and Perry Como singing to her from the radio, it was a very nearly perfect moment. At one point, he did reach over and take her hand and offered a vivid smile. She smiled back.

Thomas walked her to the door, as he always did, holding her hand the entire time. They paused at the top of the marble stairs and stood facing each other. He took both of her hands in his, suddenly looking gentle at the edges.

"I'm sorry if I upset you earlier." She didn't know what she had expected him to say, but it hadn't been that. Did she need him to apologize? To feel sorry for her? No. She tried to think of something to say.

"It wasn't your fault." Rosemary didn't like the way her voice sounded. Shaky and unsure. Vulnerable. Anger would've been easier, but that would hardly be fair to him. The desire to clench her fists arose, but he was holding her hands tightly. "I'm sorry if it ruined your day."

"Not in the least." His answer came almost too quickly, but then he smiled in a way that turned the inside of his eyebrows up. A few creases appeared in his forehead and dimples appeared on his cheeks. It was a smile that seemed far too genuine to dismiss. She couldn't help but smile back.

"All right then," she answered, "thank you for a wonderful day."

"Of course," he paused for only a moment. "You know the jazz festival is just around the corner."

"Yes. Are you going?"

"I assume you'll be there."

"Billie Holiday is performing." She said it in such a way that Thomas realized it was the only explanation he needed.

"Will you go with me?" He said it with his head tilted to the side and forward a bit as if hanging on the possibility of her answer.

"I'd love to." It was said almost without thinking, with a tone near surprise as the words left her mouth. But his smile was brilliant.

Rosemary changed quickly into casual pants and a blouse, slipping her feet into ballet flats and grabbing her bag as she ran out of the door. She had to leave the house before Hazel found her to question her about the day. She couldn't face her younger sister's wide brown eyes yet. They would be too clear and excited, ready to drink in the details of a romantic outing. And Rosemary couldn't paint such a picture before she understood it herself.

Ophelia's house looked empty when she drove up to it. There was always a look about the house when her friend wasn't home, as though it realized the emptiness. She was correct. Anthony informed her that Ophelia had gone into town for business for the afternoon. Rosemary was welcome in the house, of course, and considered waiting in Ophelia's room for her friend's return. It was something she'd done on several occasions. But not today. Not with so many thoughts and feelings bumping into each other inside her.

Instead, she went to the library and found Ophelia's copy of *The Great Gatsby* and then made her way outside.

She hadn't thought to bring her own. She'd been in too big of a hurry to leave before Hazel found her.

"I'll send some iced tea out for you, Miss Covington," Anthony said as she passed him in the hall, to which she nodded gratefully before stepping onto the verandah. The ginger-colored light fell on her surroundings in a strange way, as if illuminating them from the inside. But it was peaceful. Ophelia's house was always peaceful—as if it knew something the world didn't and because of that, it could keep you safe.

She kicked off her shoes before lounging back in a chair and allowing her worries to dissolve into the literature. Somewhere in the back of her mind, she admitted it perhaps wasn't the finest way to deal with what was bothering her, but with Ophelia gone, it seemed like the next best option.

"So we beat on, boats against the current, borne back ceaselessly into the past."

Rosemary didn't know how long she'd been reading when she suddenly heard this, but she couldn't have been more surprised when she looked up and saw Donald Jones. She must've looked as startled as she felt because he chuckled. "I didn't mean to scare you, Miss Covington. Do you mind if I join you?"

"Not at all," she answered, setting the book aside with a smile. Mr. Jones sat next to her and began pouring them both glasses of iced tea. Interestingly, Rosemary hadn't even heard the maid bring it out. She looked around her and realized it had been much longer than she'd thought.

"You seem to be enjoying yourself," he commented then, handing her the tea.

"I'm afraid I rather lost track of time," she admitted. "Understandably so, however."

"I agree," he answered, "Fitzgerald was a genius."

"You know Fitzgerald?"

"Don't look so shocked," he chuckled. "Just because I'm an accountant doesn't mean I don't enjoy good literature."

"I'm so intrigued," Rosemary laughed with him. "Tell me everything." That made him laugh harder and he shook his head.

"I love to read." He said it so simply that Rosemary couldn't help but continue to laugh. "I always have. It lets you into other people's lives, and helps you make sense of your own."

"You're more philosophical than I gave you credit for, Mr. Jones," she answered, gratefully taking advantage of the comfort the tea provided in the evening warmth.

"I'll take that as the compliment it obviously was."

"Please do."

"So why Gatsby?" he asked as he leaned back in the chair and folded his arms loosely.

"Why not?" Rosemary began, unable to hide the rising passion in her voice. "It is so obviously a classic. So completely beautiful. No matter how many times I read it, I can never stop learning from it or being impressed with its raw beauty. It's stunning."

"What is your favorite part?"

"The language," Rosemary answered without hesitation. "Fitzgerald knew how to say so much while saying so little. He could write the things most of us only ever think. He knew how to write about the soul, and our deepest thoughts and fears. He may have been writing about common things, but it wasn't common at all. Nowhere is that more prevalent than in Jay Gatsby's story. In many ways, it is a love story, and for a moment, you can't help but believe in the second chance of love. But at the same time, it is about life itself and the morals of society. It makes you question everything." He had been slowly nodding along with her during her impromptu speech as if he understood every word.

"It certainly questions traditional values," he began, "and I couldn't help but root for Gatsby and Daisy at one point. You eventually come to understand that it can't happen, that their love was perhaps more in their minds than it ever actually was. But it brings up some interesting questions."

"Isn't all love that way?" she wondered. "Don't we just make it more than it is? We see it as something huge and deeper than our bones but maybe it isn't. Maybe it is doomed to cause hurt and fail. Maybe Fitzgerald was trying to tell us something."

"You can't know anything about Fitzgerald and believe that for a second," Donald countered. "Of course he believed in love. Real love. That's why he wrote about it. Don't you believe in it?"

"Perhaps," she answered, "but why did you choose that particular quote? The one about being borne back into the past?"

"It is probably my favorite line in the novel. Which is interesting, because I don't like to think of myself as a pessimist. But there is a bit of truth there. Sometimes it feels that no matter what we do, we are slaves to what we've left behind us. I think that Gatsby would certainly agree."

"Are you a slave to what you've left behind you, Mr. Jones?" His dark eyes, which had been velvety and open, suddenly became hard. As if he was pulling all his energy back inside himself. It was an almost imperceptible shift, yet Rosemary felt the absence of him as keenly as if he'd walked away. She might have prodded him to explain it if she hadn't suddenly realized that she often did the exact same thing.

Eleven

Rosemary never did get to talk with Ophelia about what had happened with Thomas on the boat. That evening quickly melted away into another party that ended in blurry memories of too many lights and diamonds. And a longing for a scotch. But when Rosemary awoke the next morning, she couldn't decide if the boat incident was even worth bringing up. She was certain that Ophelia had better things to do with her time than constantly sort through Rosemary's feelings on her behalf.

She didn't often join her family for breakfast, but that morning she arrived just as June did. And had to laugh at her mother's overly dramatic surprise at seeing her there.

"Goodness, Rosemary! How is it that we've earned the honor of your presence at breakfast?"

"I wanted the newspaper," Rosemary answered, taking it from beside her father's plate. Arthur only pretended to be annoyed at her for it, apparently deciding to be on her side in the breakfast teasing.

"Does the front page happen to mention a certain yachting trip you conveniently forgot to tell me everything about?" Hazel asked over her piece of toast, and Rosemary couldn't help but laugh. Though her sister's voice had a thread of seriousness in it, this certainly wasn't something Rosemary was going to discuss at the breakfast table. Or anywhere else for that matter. It seemed that no matter where she turned, she was faced with the reality of her uncertainties.

"Rumor has it you've been spending time with Thomas Davenport," Arthur said as he spread orange marmalade on his toast, his eyebrows raised above his green eyes. "What can you tell me about that?"

"Yes, Rosemary, what can you tell us about that?" Hazel was clearly teasing her now, apparently sensing how uncomfortable their father's comment had made her older sister.

"I can tell you that it's true," Rosemary answered, abruptly handing the newspaper back to her father and pouring herself some tea. Arthur gazed at her for only a moment more before seemingly deciding that this was enough of an explanation for now. He may have been distant at times, but he understood his daughters very well.

"Your mother tells me that Louis has offered to find you a job," Arthur said then as he opened the newspaper. "Would you like to take him up on it?"

"I'm still thinking about it," Rosemary answered, grateful for the change in conversation. "It would be a dream come true."

"It's been so long since we were there," Hazel interjected. "Can we go to visit soon? I'm sure Uncle Louis misses us."

"Let's get the season out of the way first, Hazel," June said, obviously taking her husband's side and trying to steer the breakfast conversation into safer waters that didn't have to do with immediate decision making. Rosemary just wished that there was a way to avoid talking about it altogether. But that was never the way it worked with such things, as she well knew. There would always be a moment when one had to face the truth of everything, no matter how painful.

Thomas was about hope. Whatever else about him that confused Rosemary, she knew this. He was infuriating in the way he could smile away anything. The way he could make her forget everything with a flash of a grin and his blue eyes. He turned the world upside down and often left her in a state of exhilarated confusion. And more than once, she got the feeling that with him, she was stumbling about from one too bright moment to the next.

That's the way it was with Thomas Davenport. No matter what they did, the memory was always glazed over in a light nearly too bright to bear. It was something she had recognized about Thomas from the moment she met him: how fast and bright his world burned. And no matter what she did, perhaps because of all she did, she found herself going along with him. The harder she resisted him, the more of her mind he stole. There was a disturbing inevitability to it all, and yet Rosemary found her world illuminated in a way she'd thought was lost.

The morning of the jazz festival, she woke with stars in her eyes. Memories of the evening before flooded her mind. She and Thomas had left a party early and had gone driving along the coast, and they hadn't returned until well into the night. If she closed her eyes and concentrated, she could remember the taste of whiskey from his lips. Even if he hadn't been drinking, he always tasted a bit like whiskey.

He would be there to pick her up later in the afternoon before the program would begin in the evening. Of course, Billie Holiday wouldn't be performing until the next day, during the Sunday night program. But Rosemary couldn't help but be excited for all of it. The festival itself had caused quite a stir in Newport; a stir she realized she'd been emotionally avoiding all summer. It was as if that morning, everything came into focus, and suddenly she was awake.

It would have been impossible to not notice the hordes of people pouring into Newport—many of them younger people. The truth was that jazz wasn't entirely popular in the upper crust of society, so it didn't surprise her that many of the crowd were outsiders. She doubted she and Thomas would see many of their own circle there. When she was being honest with herself, she had to admit that therein was some of the appeal of going.

With Frank Sinatra singing in the background, Rosemary readied for the day. Ophelia had invited her over for the morning and early afternoon. There would most certainly be lunch and iced tea involved, but more than that, Rosemary knew her friend would be prodding. She wasn't entirely sure that there was much to tell, but she was delighted at the prospect of avoiding the conversation.

But perhaps Ophelia had things of her own to tell. Rosemary realized—as she gathered the last of her things and climbed into her car—that it seemed to have been weeks since she'd really spoken with her friend. Or with anybody other than Thomas, for that matter. It was almost unnerving, the way she'd been swept into such a spell, and she had to wonder what all she had missed while hiding behind too much sun.

Ophelia was waiting beside the pool, a wide hat obscuring dark sunglasses. Ralph sat in the crook of her arm. She wore a yellow bathing suit with large, white polka dots, and her bright red lips eased into a happy smile when she saw her friend.

"So you *are* still living in Newport." Her sarcasm couldn't be missed, but Rosemary simply laughed and scooped Ralph into her arms. He wasn't amused. Some days, he pretended to be good friends with her, but Rosemary was aware that Ophelia's dog merely tolerated her existence as a mundane aspect of his life.

"Well, it seems not much has changed in my apparent absence," she answered, setting Ralph down as she kicked off her sandals.

"It's kind of you to come and find out." Ophelia wasn't really upset, not with the way her blue eyes danced when she set aside her sunglasses and joined Rosemary at the edge of the pool. "But I'm afraid that in order to make up for it all, you've got some explaining to do."

"I wish I could," Rosemary said, unclipping her skirt and tossing it aside, "but I'm afraid there really isn't much to tell."

"Oh, there's plenty to tell. What you're referring to is how you keep turning it over in your head and ruining what is actually very simple."

"That's the problem, Ophelia. It should be simple. I want it to be simple. But I don't think it is. Not with Thomas."

Ophelia, much to Rosemary's dismay, nodded as though she accepted this statement. While Ophelia always understood exactly what she meant, it was rare that she didn't pose a counter-argument or press for more of Rosemary's thought process. But this time she didn't. Maybe she actually agreed with Rosemary. It seemed Ophelia understood that the closer one got to Thomas, the further away he became.

In fact, Ophelia understood a great many things about Thomas that hid behind her eyes and blurred the edges in worry. But she didn't ever say much about it because he was a world of mystery Rosemary had gotten lost in. And in so many ways, Ophelia knew that she was to blame for it. Oh, Thomas would have wormed his way into Rosemary's mind all on his own. But Ophelia had certainly helped. For many reasons, she didn't regret this; but for the wistfully lost look in her friend's dark eyes, she felt personally responsible in some way. She hadn't wanted that. Rosemary had been lost for far too long.

Twelve

Ophelia was going to the jazz festival with Donald Jones. He didn't particularly love jazz; in fact, he tried to avoid it, but Ophelia fascinated him so much that he couldn't turn down her invitation. And the festival had been talked of constantly since his arrival in Newport. He could hardly not attend at this point.

The first day of the festival was spent mostly in his office. Ophelia's project in Italy was coming to a head, and there was quite a bit of work to be done to finish things up. He finally ventured out of the house in the early afternoon. If he didn't clear his head before the festival, he doubted he'd much of a companion.

He hadn't walked very far before he heard laughter coming from the direction of Ophelia's swimming pool. He didn't have to go see who the laughter belonged to. Rosemary Covington had a laugh that couldn't have ever been mistaken for anybody else's. The thought caused a small smile to pull at the corners of his mouth.

It was one thing among many he knew for certain about her, though he'd only had a handful of conversations with her since his arrival. Donald saw a good bit of himself reflected in her amber eyes. It wasn't uncommon for the light to suddenly leave them as though a door had been slammed shut inside her mind. He'd have been insurmountably curious if he didn't know that he often did the same thing.

He wished it wasn't the case, of course, but Newport was doing strange things to him. Living amongst these people seemed to remind him of what it meant to *live*. He had realized rather suddenly some weeks before that it had been years since he'd really experienced life. He'd been running for far too long, and this trip to Newport had suddenly halted his retreat.

It was teaching him that one couldn't run from the past, and that everybody had pieces of their lives they'd prefer to keep hidden from the world. Rosemary Covington in particular seemed to be the piece of the puzzle he couldn't work out. And when he chose to dwell on it, he realized it was because she was so very much like him in many ways. He'd wondered more than once what hid behind her ready sarcasm and blunt honesty. But he imagined that she'd have to trust him to incomprehensible depths before she'd ever breathe those secrets. And trust was hard to come by. Maybe there would come a moment when he'd get the chance to tell her that he understood her better than she thought.

Though he couldn't exactly pinpoint why it should matter. She certainly seemed too wrapped up in Thomas Davenport recently to care about much else. Ophelia had commented on it more than once in a factual sort of way. As though dealing with business. But Donald was getting to know Ophelia well enough to know that she was worried about her friend. Perhaps for the reasons that Donald would never get to know. It finally seemed, however, that he wasn't the only one who understood that the subtle currents of mystery and intrigue fueling Newport couldn't go unacknowledged forever.

Rosemary left Ophelia's house with a much lighter heart than she'd had when she arrived. Excitement bubbled around the edges of her stomach, and she was trying to fight off a smile that was pulling incessantly at her mouth. She had no idea what would happen that night, if anything, but somehow, she got the feeling that everything would change. She couldn't wait to find out what it was.

After a long soak in the bath, and with her now clean hair smelling like lavender, Rosemary began the process of getting ready for the evening. She had only been sitting at her vanity for a few moments when a light tapping came at her door. She wasn't surprised in the least to see Hazel standing expectantly in the hall. Her eyes were wide in excitement. Rosemary couldn't help but laugh at the smile she wore.

"I assume this means you're here to help me get ready," she said, stepping aside so that Hazel could sweep dramatically into the room. She did notice that her sister was holding a record in her hands, and she laughed again. It would be Dean Martin. Hazel was crazy about Dean Martin. Rosemary often had to point out that it was most likely because of her own interest in Frank Sinatra. Hazel had never agreed, but it was the one argument when Rosemary invoked her privileges as the older sister.

"And by the looks of it, we've got a lot of work to do," Hazel teased as she walked to the record player and removed the ever-present Frank Sinatra record to make room for Mr. Martin.

"Do you approve of my dress?" Rosemary questioned as the music cracked and then filled the room.

"Hmm." Hazel was silent for a moment as she wandered over to where the evening dress was hanging near the closet. It was a black gown, tea-length, with a wide sweetheart neck, cap sleeves, and hugged her waist before traveling into a full skirt. She would wear simple black heels with it.

"Well?" Rosemary prodded, unnerved by Hazel's critical gaze that seemed to last far too long.

"Diamonds?" she finally asked.

"Yes," Rosemary answered with a firm nod, gesturing toward the jewelry she'd paired with the dress. "Lots and lots of diamonds."

"Oh, good," Hazel gave one of her rare nods of complete approval and began dragging an armchair across the room so that she could sit next to the vanity. Finally, she flopped into it, tossing her feet up over the side. "What's Thomas like?"

"Well, handsome, obviously. He loves baseball." Rosemary began working a brush through her curls. "And he tastes like whiskey."

"Rosemary!" Hazel's face turned bright red as she hid behind her blonde hair. It was some moments before she could collect herself enough to emerge.

"What's he *really* like?" she questioned again.

"He's funny. And smart. And very ambitious," Rosemary answered with a smile. "He likes to enjoy life."

"Does he make you happy?" Hazel's voice suddenly became strangely serious, and Rosemary didn't like it. Not when her heart was feeling so light. Not when she had so much hope for that evening.

"He's exciting. Exhilarating, even. He reminds me of what it means to truly experience life instead of hiding from it. He helps me see things differently. That's happiness, isn't it?"

"It could be."

"What are you wearing tonight?" Rosemary asked.

"Blue," Hazel answered. "Something Mother had sent up from New York. She wants me to wear pearls." She scrunched her nose at the thought.

"There's nothing wrong with pearls."

"You're right, but I've never been a fan of them. Especially on me. Dad isn't particularly excited to go. I hope he doesn't make it miserable. Maybe I'll sneak away and join you and Thomas."

"He'd be thrilled to formally meet you," Rosemary answered, "but don't sneak. Aren't any of your friends going?"

"Some. But you're the only one going who really cares about the music itself. Everybody else just sees it as another social event. I'd rather stay home and ride my horse." This didn't surprise Rosemary in the least. Hazel was a very talented rider and preferred spending time in the stables to most things. Though she didn't believe for a second that she was the only one going who cared about the music.

They stayed together most of the afternoon, Hazel eventually dragging herself out of the armchair to get ready alongside her sister. June even joined them at one point. The closer it got to the start of the evening, the more excitement began lacing itself through the air. Arthur even seemed to feel it when the three of them finally sashayed down the stairs. A rare smile lit up his green eyes.

"Have a good time tonight," he said to Rosemary before offering an arm to both June and Hazel. Rosemary couldn't help but laugh at his obvious pride.

"I'll see you all there," she called after them, watching out the window as they pulled away in the Rolls-Royce.

She wandered over to a nearby mirror then, checking her appearance one last time. Thomas would be arriving at any minute. She wanted to be absolutely sure that she looked her best. The lipstick she'd chosen for that evening was a darker red than what she usually wore, and Hazel had helped her pin her hair up in a more elaborate style than was normal for her. She smoothed her skirt one last time and concluded that she looked presentable.

Her kitten heels made clicking noises on the marble floor as she walked back toward the shining windows. The early evening sun poured through the glass and reflected on the diamonds she wore, and it made her smile to think of the jewelry. Hazel had, in fact, ended up wearing pearls. And they looked stunning on her—as Rosemary had known they would.

She smiled again at the thought and settled into a nearby chair that gave her a view of the drive. At any moment, Thomas's Corvette would arrive, the same blue as his eyes. Perhaps he'd flick away a cigarette as he approached the door, having taken one long drag from it. He'd be wearing a dazzling smile.

But Thomas never came. She might have begun to worry that something had happened to him. But somehow, she knew he was safe. Somehow, she knew that wasn't the problem. Rosemary stood in the entryway, looking outside, and realized that something between them had finally shifted into its inescapable place. She had sensed it but refused to acknowledge it. And now it stared her right in the eyes. The reality of everything she'd known all along.

Eventually, Rosemary wandered out to her Jaguar, the deep pine green looked blue under the night sky. Everything was bleeding an inevitable shade of blue. Her skirt made delicate swishing sounds that were far too cheery as she slid into the leather seat and started the car. She felt oddly indifferent, and yet somehow raw. But everything was painfully clear. A great curtain had been removed from her eyes and suddenly, she could really see. Suddenly, everything made sense.

It didn't take long for her to drive to his house, and when she arrived there, all of the huge windows stared back at her blankly. All except one. One lone window on the bottom floor was trying desperately to emit the light from a lamp, but it was so weak as to be pathetic.

The front door swung open easily at her touch, and she stepped onto the marble tiles slowly. Her eyes adjusted to the gloom only to find two suitcases next to the door, a traveling jacket draped over them. The tinkling of a glass then jerked her from this sight, and she followed the sound into the nearby library.

Thomas was sitting in a dark corner, somehow more obscured in the light of the lamp. He was wearing his tuxedo. But the jacket was discarded on the floor as if roughly tossed there, and the bow tie was haphazardly undone. His hair was sticking out a bit. As if he'd been pulling on it. A glass was perched in his hand and a nearly empty bottle of whiskey sat next to him on a table.

"Rosemary…" She couldn't decide if she was surprised or not when he spoke first.

"I waited for you." Her voice was much stronger than she expected. But the words weren't what she wanted to say. She didn't know what she wanted to say.

"I know." He drained the glass and poured himself another, which he also drained. "I know." All of their words came out blunt and heavy like a storm of bricks.

She stepped closer to where he sat, forcing him to look at her. He could only meet her eyes for a moment before getting to his feet unsteadily and retrieving a second glass. He poured it full of whiskey and placed it in her hand, as though not really thinking. She looked down at the liquid. Swished it around in the glass. He saw her beginning to lift it to her lips, but stopped her suddenly and emptied it himself.

"I won't let that be my doing. Along with everything else."

Rosemary looked into his eyes then and wanted to feel a million things passing between them. But she didn't. Because there was nothing there. And they both knew it. She pressed her eyes shut, and let the realization of everything prickle into tears. But they didn't fall. They merely pooled at the edges of her eyes and burned hot.

"I guess you'll be going then." She couldn't keep the sound of her tears from her voice. But there was no need. He could see it. He knew.

"Yes." His voice was raspy. He very suddenly turned then and threw the glass at the wall.

It shattered into fragments that couldn't capture the light of the lamp. She didn't even flinch, but he pushed a hand into his hair, pulling at it. "Rosemary, I…please…"

"Thomas." Suddenly, her voice was extremely tired. "Wasn't it always going to end this way?"

"I didn't want it to!" He sounded as though everything he felt was in a battle to get out, and it lost. "But I can't. I can't be what you think I am. Or what you need me to be. I just can't."

"I know." She watched as he shakily pulled out a cigarette from his silver case. His hands were unsteady as he lit it and took a long drag. And then one more.

"Goodbye." He lifted his hand to touch her cheek, but it was so light that she hardly felt it.

Thirteen

Thomas Davenport left Newport as quickly and mysteriously as he had entered it. And it wasn't hard for the majority of people to put together that something had happened between him and Rosemary Covington. The problem was that nobody knew what, and with a somewhat generous portion of the season still left, there would be no escaping the questioning glances and whispers.

But Rosemary had no answers to give them. Even if it were their business. All she knew was that he was gone, and he'd left behind him an ache that spread all over her skin. Her mind was strangely empty. She had no questions. She needed no answers. There was a finality in his leaving, an understanding. But still the dull ache.

June stayed with her that first night. The moment Rosemary stumbled back into the house, her mother was instantly by her side. She hadn't known that her family was home, but no doubt June had put all the pieces together. And the next thing Rosemary knew, she was being led to her room and put into her pajamas as if she were a doll. Her mother tucked her in bed and turned on the Frank Sinatra record, sitting with her daughter in the cool darkness until she fell asleep.

The first thing Rosemary saw when she opened her eyes the next morning was sunlight illuminating the edges of her chiffon curtains. It was pale yellow and fell on the carpet in soft rays. But somehow it was also brilliant, illuminating, and pure. It was as if even the sun had woken up. And it was shining.

She pulled the down-filled blankets back from around her and padded quietly over to the window. The morning air poured on her skin when she opened it: crisp and cool. Below her, the lawn was still, and beyond that, the sun fell on the rest of the world. Everything was simple and nice as if it had been washed clean. Even the light looked clearer. The thought made her smile.

She was distracted from these thoughts when the telephone rang. There was only one person it could've been.

"Yes?"

"Rosemary?" Ophelia's voice held more worry than it had in years. The memories of the last time she'd heard it hurt far worse than what she felt at that moment.

"Yes, Ophelia. I'm here." Rosemary slid into her silk robe and pushed the sleeves up past her elbows before sinking into a chair.

"Thomas is gone, isn't he?" The line cracked a bit, and because of it, Rosemary couldn't place her friend's tone of voice.

"Yes. Yes, he is." There was silence for a moment, and then Ophelia let out a long breath.

"I'm so sorry, Rosemary." For a heart-wrenching moment, Rosemary almost felt the pain Ophelia thought she felt. But there was none. "This is my fault. I'm the one who told you to take a leap. I'm the one who told you to try again."

"Please don't blame yourself," Rosemary answered, gripping the telephone until her knuckles turned white. "This isn't your fault. We all knew it would happen this way."

"How…how are you?"

"Empty," Rosemary admitted, pushing her curls away from her face, "but not in pain."

She only cried once. Hazel brought her tea one night, two days after Thomas had left. For some reason, it was this that undid Rosemary. Hazel was always so vibrant and alive, so brilliantly young. Her sympathy was more than Rosemary knew how to bear. The evening ended with her younger sister holding her in her arms as she wept the tears of broken hopes. Rosemary came to understand that these were not the type of tears that came from depth. Those she had felt before. These were the kind that lived on the surface and broke when the maybes did. And when they were all dried up, they never came back.

Though the whispers were, in fact, inescapable. Rosemary braved a party as soon as one could be found, just to prove that she could. Just to understand that the emptiness didn't have as much power as everybody assumed. But what Rosemary didn't expect to experience were a few kind smiles. Sympathetic eyes. Of course, there were the smirks and rude smiles. But those didn't hurt. She learned how to maneuver past it, just as the emptiness slowly worked its way out of her.

Late one evening after returning home from a party, Rosemary headed straight for the telephone in her father's study. It was generally the best place for private conversations. Some moments later, she finally heard her Uncle Louis's voice on the other end of the line. It was more of a comfort than she expected.

"Rosemary! How's my gorgeous girl?" His voice was incredibly jovial, but she had to remind herself that he had just begun his day while she was ending hers extremely late. He'd always been a person eager to start the morning.

"I'm doing well," Rosemary responded though she knew she wouldn't get away with telling that lie. She was correct.

"It sounds to me as if you aren't, my dear." The line cracked a bit. "Why else would you be phoning me at three in the morning from across the world?"

"To ask you if you'd still be willing to find me a job in London."

"Of course!" His answer was immediate and backed with a great deal of enthusiasm. "I'll begin today. Are you sure this is something you really want?" She waited for him to finish his thought, which he eventually did softly. "Are you sure you aren't running away from anything?"

"I could be," she admitted, "but I'm not going to ruin my resolve by dwelling on the possibility. It's an incredible opportunity whether or not I'm running from anything. I want to take it and move forward."

"Then I'll begin immediately." He had always had a huge amount of trust in her, believing everything she said. She wished she had his faith. "Is there anything else I can do to help you?"

"Pray," Rosemary responded. "I think I'll start doing a lot more of that myself."

Fourteen

Ophelia looked like the picture of innocence in a yellow tea-length dress and a strand of pearls. When she turned her head just right, Rosemary couldn't tell where the sunshine ended and her hair began. She had to smile and shake her head as she poured herself more tea. It didn't matter that she and Ophelia were like sisters. There was something about her friend she'd never be able to understand. No matter what she went through, a certain innocence always clung to her. An unmistakable grace. It was her most enviable quality.

"I know you love coming here for the tea," Ophelia interrupted her thoughts, "but is it too early for a gin?" Rosemary had to laugh and gestured to the nearest waiter, who nodded at her and went back into the hotel. They came often enough that it was known exactly what she meant. It wasn't long before he reemerged with Ophelia's drink on a silver tray, the sunlight glinting off the clear glass and the slice of lime bobbing at the surface.

"Tell me about the work you've been doing this summer," Rosemary requested, stirring the cream and sugar into her tea. "You rarely talk to me about your business."

"That's because most of it is unbearably dull," Ophelia answered, arching her eyebrow in interest. "Why do you ask?"

"You've never had an accountant bring the work to you before. And it's no secret that I've been distracted this summer. Too distracted, it seems, to care about your business. I'm sorry, Ophelia." Rosemary offered her the tray of cucumber sandwiches.

"There's nothing to be sorry for," Ophelia said, "but if you really are interested, I'll tell you that business is actually going very smoothly. Donald is a genius. I bought a new house just outside of Rome, and he's been handling all of it."

"Another investment?" It was uncommon for Ophelia to simply buy homes, but it would make sense if it was for that purpose.

"Yes," she answered, gesturing for the waiter to have another gin on the way. "It's a sort of dream, I guess. It has been exciting."

"It isn't like you to be so sentimental when it comes to business," Rosemary observed. "It seems like it isn't so much a business venture as an emotional one."

"Yes, well, it was something Mother always wanted to do."

Rosemary couldn't hide her surprise. Or the pain that stabbed her heart on behalf of her friend. Ophelia rarely talked about her parents, and when she did, a strangely thin veil fell over her blue eyes.

"Oh, yes," she answered quietly, "I should have known. I remember how much she loved Italy."

"And Shakespeare." Rosemary almost couldn't bear the faraway look on Ophelia's face. For a moment, she began to worry that there was much more here than her friend was letting on.

"Are you all right, Ophelia?" She knew that her voice conveyed what she really meant. And it wasn't a friendly question one asked in passing. But she didn't get an answer until Ophelia had finished her drink and shifted Ralph from one arm to the other.

"Honestly, Rosemary, I've never been happier. This project has been so good for me, and for the first time in a long time, I'm excited about something," she paused a moment. "The only thing that could make me any happier would be to see you happy. Not floating on the surface of a maybe happy, but really, truly happy."

It was the perfect way to describe what her time with Thomas had been. A maybe. She shook her head and finished her tea, content to let the thoughts melt away. It was strange, how it was so recently over, and yet it also felt as though it had never happened.

"I called Uncle Louis a few days ago. I asked him to find me a job after all."

"And?"

"He told me he'd begin immediately. And also asked me if I was running from anything." The ocean breeze picked up a bit as Rosemary answered, blowing a curl across her eyes and making it impossible for her to read Ophelia's gaze. She didn't question further, though, which led Rosemary to believe that she understood.

"I think it will be a dream come true for you," Ophelia finally said. "You were made to walk the streets of a different city than this one. Your family may belong here, but you don't. You never have." She said it very matter-of-factly because they both knew it was true.

"And what about you?" Rosemary questioned. "Will you be moving to this new house in Rome?" Although she would miss her friend terribly, the idea of Ophelia off on such an exciting adventure was a beautiful one. If anybody deserved that kind of happiness, it was her.

"Yes," she answered simply, "as soon as all my business affairs are in order. I'm not sure how permanent it will be, but for now, I'm just excited about the whole idea. On the bright side, we'll still be in the same half of the planet." That made Rosemary laugh, and Ophelia grinned back.

"I wish you'd teach me to be as marvelous as you," Rosemary said then.

Ophelia winked, "If you haven't learned by example yet then there's not much that I can do for you."

With the jazz festival behind them, the Newport crowd put their full attention to the normal parties and outings of the season. There was always something to do, always somebody to see. The strangest thing about it was that none of it bothered Rosemary as much now. Because as the days melted away, she found herself looking more and more forward to moving to England. Uncle Louis would insist she live with him, of course, but perhaps after some time, she'd get her own place there. London had always felt like home whenever she visited it. Something whispered to her that if she were to chase this dream, she'd go there and never return. And perhaps that was exactly what needed to happen.

Several days later, on an oddly warm afternoon, Rosemary climbed into her Jaguar and left the Covington mansion behind her. The first instinct was usually to go to Ophelia's, but somehow she found herself at a bookstore in the city. The second that she walked into the store, she felt a calmness close over her. It was moments like these where she often wondered why she spent so much time amongst tinkling glass when a room full of books was all that she needed to feel whole.

"Miss Covington," the storekeeper addressed her with a voice that indicated he knew she had money and expected her to spend it. "Can I help you find anything?" Rosemary tossed him a smile, deciding not to let his tone ruin the temporary peace she had walked into.

"Fitzgerald," she answered and sighed gratefully when he led her to a nearby shelf. She was even more grateful when he left her there in peace.

Rosemary was unsure of how long she stood there, completely mesmerized by a beautifully bound copy of *The Beautiful and the Damned*. It never mattered that she had copies of all of Fitzgerald's literature. She could never seem to get enough of his words. Each time she opened a book of his, it felt like a completely new experience. As if she'd find something new in the pages. Some sort of answer, perhaps.

"Mr. Jones!" The front door of the store opened and closed rather abruptly, jerking Rosemary into the reality beyond the pages. She couldn't see Donald Jones walking into the store from where she stood, but she knew it was him before she heard his reply.

"Mr. Harris." The tone in Donald's voice seemed familiar somehow. But she couldn't place it. "Do you have anything new in today?"

"Exhausted your library again?"

"It would seem so." Tired, Rosemary realized then. He sounded tired. She recognized the tone because she was feeling the same way herself. It was a deeper tiredness. She wondered what had brought that sound into his voice.

"Mr. Harris." Rosemary came out from behind the shelf then, holding the book in her hands and approaching the counter, "I'll take this, please." Donald smiled when he saw her, and the edges of his dark eyes lit up in surprise. She smiled and nodded in greeting as she silently paid for her book, ignoring Mr. Harris's obvious annoyance that she'd only purchased one.

"I'm sorry to say that I have nothing new in, Mr. Jones," Mr. Harris said then. "But maybe you'd like to look around regardless. You can always find something new."

"Maybe Miss Covington has a few suggestions," Donald answered, looking at her with raised eyebrows and a silent invitation.

"Well, of course," Rosemary answered, leading Donald away from the counter and into the maze of shelves. Anything to get away from the disapproving looks of Mr. Harris, who quite obviously thought he knew much more about her than he did. No doubt it had something to do with Thomas. The thought brought a sigh to her lips that she pushed away. It would be so much easier to leave Thomas where he belonged once everybody stopped reminding her about him with their stares.

"Escaping?" Donald asked, his voice suddenly light with suppressed laughter.

"Is it that obvious?"

"Maybe just to me. Was there really a book back here you wanted to show me?" he gestured to the atlases they were surrounded with.

"Have you really exhausted the library at your guesthouse?" This time he did laugh and shake his head.

"All right, so we're both escaping. Let's do it someplace else, then."

"Like where?"

"A diner, obviously. We're both in need of a milkshake."

Fifteen

When his smile was genuine, his eyes became slits and crinkled at the corners. And a dimple appeared in the top of his cheek. Just under the corner of his right eye. Rosemary noticed this several days later as they spent the afternoon in the library of Ophelia's guest cottage, sharing a pitcher of iced tea and pouring over the books.

"What's your favorite book?" Donald asked from where his head was buried in a shelf. "Fitzgerald aside. What besides his works?"

"Pride and Prejudice," Rosemary admitted sheepishly. "I can't help myself. It's just too beautiful."

"I've never read it."

"Well, you should," she answered as she climbed up a nearby ladder. "What about you? What's your favorite book?"

"I'm pleased to announce that I recently finished *Les Misẽrables*, and enjoyed it immensely. I've always wanted to read it and finally did. In only a week, I might add."

"I'm intrigued. Tell me everything."

"Haven't you read it?" His soft eyes were wide in exasperation. He seemed to think that because she had a degree in journalism, she had read all of the classics of the world. She decided to pretend that was the case, even if she'd eventually have to tell him the truth.

"I do have a degree in journalism, Donald."

"Oh, of course." He accepted her half-truth too easily, and it made her smile. She made a mental note to correct it at some point.

"What is it that you love most about *Les Misẽrables*?" Rosemary asked, momentarily distracted by a Tolstoy hidden on the shelf next to her. "Hugo is brilliant, of course, but didn't you find him slightly longwinded?"

"Oh, definitely," Donald answered without hesitation. "But that is part of what makes it so amazing. You learn everything there is to know about every character. You're never left guessing."

"But isn't that what is great about literature?" she asked. "You're supposed to be left guessing sometimes, to be able to determine what it means to you personally. Right?"

"Maybe." His voice was teasing as he said it, and it made her smile. "Have you ever thought of writing a novel, Rosemary?"

"Many times. I've even begun several, mostly back in my university years."

"Why didn't you ever finish one?"

"I suppose because I knew I'd never be a match for Hugo." That made him laugh, which was beginning to be a very pleasant sound. She smiled at that thought and settled comfortably into one of the leather armchairs, her tea easily within reaching distance.

"Tolstoy!" His voice seemed genuinely upset at seeing the book she'd picked, but she was learning things about him much too quickly to believe for one moment that his emotions went beyond disbelief. "Here you are lecturing me on the greatest writer in the world, and then sit with a Tolstoy. It is common knowledge that Tolstoy is the Hugo of Russia. Hardly original."

"You're entitled to your opinion, of course," she answered, laughing with him before wandering over to the record player in the corner. "What records does Ophelia have in here?"

"Why music? We're in the middle of a heated intellectual debate." His voice held a tone far too light to indicate a debate of any kind.

"Always music, Donald. If you learn this now, your life will be much easier. Oh, here we go. She's always prepared with Frank Sinatra on hand."

"You're a fan of Sinatra's?" He'd wandered over to the pile of books she'd picked out, eyeing them with a curious glance.

"To put it mildly." She adjusted the volume slightly and wandered back over to her chair. "You mean to say that you aren't?"

"Not particularly." There wasn't a hint of regret in his dark eyes, and for some reason, it made her smile.

"We'll have to fix that." She said it in such a way that indicated there wasn't room for debate, but he gave her a smile that said he wouldn't give in that easily.

They began going on what he termed "adventures." These escapades were usually spontaneous. He would phone her in the late afternoon, his voice sounding bored as if he'd had too many numbers but excited as if he couldn't wait to get somewhere. She had only to pick up the telephone with a brief greeting before he would say, "Let's go on an adventure." He'd arrive at the Covington mansion moments later, and off they would go.

More often than not, they ended up at a diner. It appeared he had found his favorite one in the area fairly quickly. Donald was crazy about hamburgers. He talked endlessly about how they were the one thing missing from the life of the rich crowd.

"Don't get me wrong, Newport society has its advantages. But you can only eat so many fancy meals before you go crazy. Don't you ever just need this?" He asked this as he piled grilled onions on his burger, and Rosemary couldn't help but laugh. The truth was that she did need it, and they missed a significant amount of season events as they spent their evenings in diners and conversation. She regretted none of it.

But when it came right down to it, Rosemary found her emotions regarding Donald Jones hard to sort out. It would have been ridiculous to ignore how well they got along, and yet there was something there that she couldn't see. And while part of her hid itself away trying to sort that out, the rest of her began spending more and more time with him.

Perhaps what Rosemary enjoyed most about Donald Jones was the fact that no matter how much they talked, there always seemed to be something else to say. Even in the moments when the words ran dry, being with him in silence wasn't uncomfortable. It was almost as though they could speak without really speaking. She'd often wondered if such a thing were actually possible.

But then again, she'd often wondered a great many things that Donald either solved or coaxed out of her. He had a strange habit of being able to make her say things she'd become an expert at hiding. Her secrets rose to the surface in his presence, as if all he had to do was be near her in order for her to understand that she could speak them. That it was safe to do so. Perhaps it was this that caused her nervousness. These very realities made him more dangerous than Thomas had ever been.

Rosemary tried to avoid thinking of Thomas, or of comparing the two men. But with the two experiences so close together, it was nearly impossible not to do the latter. And as for the former, there was to be no escaping reminders of what had happened earlier in the summer. Even though in many ways it felt as though it had never happened to her, but somebody else in a completely different life. Nevertheless, she couldn't be seen anywhere without the whispers. And now that she was being seen with Donald, there was even more fuel for gossip. It had been a long time since she'd experienced such a thing. And those memories were not pleasant ones.

She wasn't surprised when Donald finally asked her about it, a few weeks after their encounter at the bookstore. They were sitting on the beach, toes buried in the sand. Donald had brought a cooler of sodas that sat between them. The only thing missing was music. She smiled at the thought and watched Donald snap open a soda, tossing the cap back into the cooler before handing her the chilled glass bottle.

"Tell me about Thomas Davenport." He requested it very simply, cracking open his own soda and taking a swig.

"What do you want to know?" she asked, once again surprised that it felt so easy to talk about. It didn't ache anymore—that had stopped long ago, but she had expected some sort of tilt inside her. Some sort of reminder of those broken hopes. But there was none.

"Were you in love with him?"

"I think I wanted to be." The honesty made her voice crack, and she realized she was much too used to keeping things like this hidden.

"But?"

"It was never about that with Thomas," she answered, pausing to drink her soda. "It was about hope. He was a maybe. Something that could've happened, but wouldn't have continued to be as brilliant as it was all the time. He was too bright. Too exhilarating. Too much."

"And?" It was beginning to be annoying, how he knew when she was still holding something back.

"And unsafe." There was something in that word "unsafe" that softened Donald's eyes as if he knew exactly what she meant. And she meant something much deeper than just being afraid to take a risk.

He looked down at her hands then, and she realized that she had them clenched. He reached over to smooth them out, and then pulled his hands away. "Why do you do that?"

"It's a nervous habit," she answered quickly, intimidated that he'd noticed. Though the truth was that she did it more often out of fear than nerves. And the way he could see past her carefully constructed exterior was certainly frightening.

He wasn't going to ask her more about it then, she could sense that, but something passed between them that convinced her he knew. Perhaps it was the simple smile he gave her just before he took his glasses off to clean them.

But he knew. And that in itself was something quite different.

"How blind are you?" she suddenly asked, taking his glasses from him before he could put them back on his face. She held them up to her own eyes for only a second before returning them, shaking her head in disbelief. It made him laugh.

"All right, one last question about Mr. Davenport."

"Are you writing a book?" she teased, which made him laugh again. "Okay, then. Just one more."

"I know you've noticed people gossiping about you. Thinking they know everything that happened," he said, "Does that hurt?"

"Not so much the fact that they talk about me. I'll admit it's been a while since I was the topic of everybody's conversation, but that doesn't bother me as much as the fact that they think they know what happened," she answered. "All of us have things that we'd rather not say, that we'd like to keep hidden. I think it's probably one of humanity's greatest sins that we all think we can look at another person and decide for them what their life is like. Until we get close enough, we really have no idea."

"Now I'm beyond intrigued. What other secrets do you have?" His tone of voice was playful, but yet she knew that he'd absorbed everything she said and agreed with it.

"I think I've told you enough for one day. But no doubt you'll get more out of me later."

Rosemary couldn't help but laugh as she said it, and he didn't disagree. He only gave her a knowing smile.

Sixteen

Two days later, Rosemary walked into the cool darkness of her father's study at his request. It was later in the morning, but the soft light hadn't quite lit up the corners of the room. She smiled at the smell, a mixture of paper and pipe tobacco.

"Your uncle is on the telephone for you," Arthur said, squeezing her shoulder as he walked past her to give her some privacy. But he stopped unexpectedly, concern suddenly in his eyes. "Are you…well?"

"Yes, Dad," she said, surprised that her eyes began burning. It was rare that he showed such tenderness toward her. "I don't know what you've heard, but believe me. I'm all right. Better than all right."

"I'm glad to hear that," he said, tugging on the end of one of her curls as he left. He hadn't done that since she was a little girl.

"Rosemary!" Uncle Louis's voice was as jovial as ever when she picked up the telephone. It made her smile.

"Hello," she said, settling into the chair behind her father's desk. "How is London today?"

"Sunny. Much more so than usual," he answered. "I'm having my tea now and looking out on the street. It's quite delightful. When are you going to join me?"

"I assume that's what you've called to talk about, isn't it?"

"Oh, yes, of course." His teasing had always held a very childlike quality that made the world seem better. "I do apologize that it's taken me some time. It wasn't for lack of offers, though. Many newspapers wanted your employment once I began looking, but I had to narrow it down to the best ones."

"And what have you found?" she questioned.

"There are at least three papers worth your closer inspection. I think it would be best if you came here first and then decided which job you'd like to take. How does that sound to you?"

"Exciting," Rosemary answered. "When would you expect me?"

"Well, I couldn't ask you to be here before the end of the season. Finish it out, return to New York with your family, and then make arrangements to come. I wouldn't be in too much of a hurry if I were you. It's a big decision you're making."

"All right then," she said. "That will be the plan for now. Enjoy your tea."

"I will, of course. Where are you going to today?"

"On an adventure."

Donald smiled when he saw her coming out of the house; the smile that crinkled his eyes. He got out of the car to open the door for her, revealing his blue jeans and a white T-shirt under a gabardine jacket.

"You're looking very James Dean today," Rosemary commented as she slid onto the leather seat.

"I'll take that as a compliment." His voice held a strange tone, and it made her laugh.

"Please do," she said, setting her handbag on the seat next to her after retrieving her sunglasses from it. They were light pink with subtle cat-like eyes. "That's how it was meant. Don't you like James Dean?"

"He's a little too…hip for me to be a fan," he said, climbing back into the driver's seat. "But since you meant it kindly, we'll move on. I assume you'd like to hear the radio." He turned the knobs until music began snapping into the air. She had to smile at him.

"However did you get away from your employer this morning?" She asked this as they drove away, the gravel of the drive slightly tossed by the wheels.

"Miss Baxter does allow me some freedom," he bantered in return, "though it isn't often. I am completely grateful to her, of course."

"Of course," she repeated with a laugh. "How is Ophelia's business going? She told me some time ago about her project in Rome. Is that what you've mainly been helping with?"

"Mostly," he confirmed, "though we have been doing some work with her family holdings in South Carolina."

"She isn't selling, is she?" The very idea seemed preposterous.

"No, but why the surprise?"

"It has to do with her parents," Rosemary said. "Her mother grew up there. Her father went to South Carolina for family business. That's how they met. They were married at the plantation, and it was left to them by Ophelia's grandparents."

"So why Rome?"

"It was a dream of her mother's. Rachel loved classic literature, particularly Shakespeare."

"I'd have never guessed," he mused lightly, and it made her smile.

"She always wanted a family home in Italy. In fact, Ophelia's father Daniel was arranging it when they were both killed." It had been so long since Rosemary had thought about it, and that made her feel guilty. No matter how far Ophelia had come, she surely thought of it daily. "They were in South Carolina visiting Rachel's parents when it happened. They were at a charity event. Ophelia was at the plantation waiting for them to come home. But they were in an accident and died instantly."

"And Anthony?" Of course, he knew that there was more to the story.

"Anthony's family has been in service to Ophelia's for generations. In a way they grew up together," Rosemary answered. "They are both the only ones left now. I think he stays with her because that is just the way it has to be. It's almost as though they are all they both have left of everything behind them." Despite the racial tensions that fueled society, there was no other reason for Anthony to remain in service. He could've done so much more. It was the same story for too many.

"But you and Ophelia have known each other all your lives," Donald stated. "She knows that she has you, too."

"It's more like I have her," she admitted. "She spends too much time solving my problems and not enough time enjoying the happiness she deserves."

"You don't give yourself enough credit." There was a note of finality in his voice, so she decided to let him win that point.

"So what's on the adventure agenda today?" Rosemary asked then, turning up the volume on the radio as one of her favorite songs began playing. Donald teasingly turned it back down just a bit before he answered.

"I thought we'd go see that new movie that came out around the time of the jazz festival. The musical."

"Oh, you mean *Seven Brides for Seven Brothers*," she said. "I didn't know you liked musicals."

"That's the one," he answered. "It's been fairly popular. And as far as I'm concerned, musicals contain the only music worth listening to." He seemed to be half-serious and half-teasing. It made her laugh, and she turned the radio back up.

There weren't many people in the theater, but Rosemary was grateful for that. It meant they could enjoy the film in peace. There wouldn't have to be as much worry about the gossip. Though why she should worry, she didn't know, because Donald certainly didn't. He paid for their tickets and an almost grotesquely large bag of popcorn with his delighted smile.

It was a different sort of smile than his truly genuine one. His eyes still crinkled and the dimple still appeared, but something that could only be described as delight radiated out of him. In a way it was childlike, and as Rosemary smiled back and walked with him into the theater, she felt a strange tug at her heart. It would've felt like sadness if the tug hadn't turned upwards.

They settled into their seats, and soon thereafter, the theater grew dark. "I just now realized I should've rethought this," Donald whispered. "I've never liked westerns."

"Don't worry. I'm not sure you can count this as a typical western."

"What a relief," he answered. "I completely forgot to even wonder if I'd like it."

"It is moments of obviousness like these when I wonder if you really are a grown man," she whispered back. "Are you sure you're 25?"

"Officially. But I'm convinced I never made it past the age of nine." It made Rosemary laugh so, that they got a disapproving look from an older woman seated some rows ahead of them. "Stop acting so barbaric or they'll throw us out. Here, eat some popcorn." Luckily, the opening music of the film began, obscuring Rosemary's further laughter.

They sat in silence for the first several moments, both of them absorbing the film and silently filing away things that they could discuss later. One of which was that it wasn't really a western in the typical matter, just as she had suspected. These thoughts were interrupted, however, when the main character Adam so quickly asked Millie to marry him. Neither of them could keep quiet.

"I guess when you know, you know." His voice was only a bit sarcastic.

"How can she possibly see anything genuine about this proposal?" Rosemary was only slightly serious. But it seemed that they were too used to having in-depth conversations about literature to sit back and enjoy a simple musical. They kept thinking of arguments to whisper back and forth. At one point, Rosemary didn't think she'd ever been as frightened as when the older woman once again turned around to glare in their direction.

The popcorn didn't last long. As soon as Donald had finished eating most of it, he reached over and took Rosemary's hand, their fingers lacing together. It was a very simple gesture, commonplace even, but her stomach flipped so violently that she was sure her entire body moved. Her first reaction was to clench her fists, which she couldn't do with him holding her hand. But then a much deeper voice of reason hushed her, breathing something deep and true into her heart. And with it, a rare peace enveloped her. She squeezed his hand a little tighter.

Seventeen

"How much longer will you be in Newport?" Rosemary asked him this later that night. They were sitting in the car, with the top down, the engine gently purring as they looked out over the ocean. The radio was playing but it wasn't loud, only a soft hum in the background. The sun was steadily retreating, brilliant hues of orange and red surrendering to the blue night.

"Until the end of the season, or as long as Ophelia needs me," he answered. "Why?"

"Just curious," she replied, though the truth was that as they'd been talking, he had let go of her hand only to start tracing circles on her palm with the tips of his fingers. The result was the complete scattering of any of her logical thoughts as well as the ability to think them.

"I need to ask you a question about Fitzgerald," Donald said then, surprising her.

"All right," she laughed. "I'm pretty sure we've exhausted the topic on several occasions. But go on."

"Why his works specifically?" he wondered. "They never have happy endings. The love always fades or ends brutally. Everyone just sort of disappears. Yet you're always talking about how beautiful all of it is. Why?"

"Because…" she had to pause and think a moment, having never understood just how right he was. Why indeed? "I think it is because I can understand where he seems to be coming from." She nodded as if to confirm to herself that this was correct. "Fitzgerald loved his wife so much, for example, and yet their marriage was marked by tragedy. When they first started going together, she suddenly decided it wasn't going to work and broke with him. He did everything he could to win her back, though she soon realized she'd made a mistake and agreed to marry him. Their love was so intense, so real, and yet they didn't get a happy ending. Zelda ended up in asylums and clinics and Fitzgerald died alone." Even though Rosemary knew the story of the Fitzgeralds, it had never hurt her heart before.

"Go on," Donald prodded.

"Well, Fitzgerald knew what it was like to experience that once-in-a-lifetime magic that everybody searches for. But he also knew what society could do, and how life can rip it away so easily. And I think that novel after novel, he tried to reconcile this and he couldn't seem to. Maybe he longed for the happy ending but didn't know how to write it." Rosemary let out a long breath, "And I guess that every time I read his books, I read them hoping his characters, as complex and real as they are, will get the endings they desire. But they never do."

"So what you're telling me is that you admire a writer who couldn't let any of his characters have a happy ending. And you think it's beautiful." He grinned as he said it, the childlike smile, and she couldn't help but grin back.

"I've always thought so!" she admitted incredulously. "I assumed there was so much beauty in tragedy because it was real. But I'm beginning to find that there is quite a bit of reality in happiness as well."

"Hmm. Who knew?" he said lightly, and she had to laugh.

"Oh, stop it," she bantered. "You're one to talk."

He honestly couldn't argue with that, and so laughed softly in agreement and then gently let go of her hand. She thought for a moment that he might shift the car into gear and drive them home, but instead, he put his arm around her and requested very simply, "Come here."

She didn't need any further invitation to scoot closer and lay her head on his chest. He wrapped his free arm around her and they sat like that in silence for just a moment. She could hear his heartbeat beside her ear. Perhaps a bit faster than normal, but mostly steady. Before she knew it, she let out a long sigh and closed her eyes, distantly shocked at how completely safe she felt.

"Don't fall asleep," he teased.

"I'm not."

"I'm pretty sure your eyes are closed."

"This just feels nice," she answered, and felt a smile tug at her mouth when she heard his heart speed up a bit.

"Oh, good." After a moment of listening to his steady breath, Rosemary began to fear that she might actually fall asleep. The peace that had fallen over her at the movie theater had yet to leave. But she didn't want to sleep, she wanted to drink in every single moment. And was grateful that she'd learned how.

"All right, so explain your love of Hugo," she requested. "He certainly wasn't about to give his characters happy endings. *Les Misérables* is one of the greatest tragedies ever written. So why that story?"

"Because it's about bravery." Apparently, he'd already prepared his response. "It doesn't end well for most of the characters, but every one of them is faced with a moment when they could let fear ruin them. They all have a choice at some point. And they decide to do what they know is right, even if they are scared. Even if they aren't sure they can do it. Even if they want to run. They continue anyway despite their fear, to create a life they know they can have."

"Now *that's* beautiful," she whispered, and she felt him smile into her hair.

Donald didn't drive her home until the moon was high in the sky. It was just a sliver of milky white, surrounded by hopeful stars. But even as late as it was, and the fact that they'd spent the entire day together, Rosemary was loathe to go back inside and watch him drive away.

"I don't…" He had been walking her to the door, but suddenly stopped and turned to her, taking both of her hands. His eyebrows were drawn down, creating a crease in his forehead. She could tell he knew what he wanted to say but was hesitant about saying it. Perhaps worried about her response. "I don't want to say goodbye."

"Perfect," she breathed a deep sigh of relief and led him away from the front door. "Neither do I."

"Where are we going?" He said it in a hushed laugh.

"I'll show you. We're almost there." The gravel drive disappeared around the corner of the house, what it led to obscured by trees. But it didn't take long to arrive at the end of it, and at the garage. It was a long, thin building with a series of big doors, and filled with a pristine line of shiny cars.

"Quite the collection." Donald was appropriately impressed, and it made her shake her head. It seemed that in some ways, all men were alike.

"A little hobby of my father's," Rosemary answered as they visited each car so he could admire it. "It was one of my favorite places when I was little, when we'd come up for the season. Father used to work out here quite a bit with the mechanics, making sure all of the cars were in perfect condition. I'd sit on a stool and eat penny candy while I watched."

"And Hazel?"

"Practically raised in the barn. Mother always rode, and Hazel takes after her." It was quite dark in the garage—the row of windows along the back wall did little when the moon wasn't very bright. But still, she knew he was smiling. She grinned and left him to admire the Rolls-Royce while she walked to where she knew there was a kerosene lamp. She didn't dare turn on all of the huge overhead lights. That would certainly attract attention.

"I can't hold your hand if you're all the way over there." Donald called over, and she laughed if only to cover up how lightheaded that made her feel.

"I'll be right back," she assured him, pulling the lamp out from under the workbench and lighting it quickly. She stopped momentarily at her Jaguar, pulling out a blanket she kept in it and walking back over to him. The flame of the lamp made a homey circle of light around them as they spread the blanket on the floor and leaned their backs against one of the cars. They sat in silence for some time, listening to the breeze blow a tree branch against a window, and some of the cars creak. But silence between them was never strained. They were quite good at simply being.

"Am I going to get you into all sorts of trouble?" he eventually asked.

"Most definitely," she answered, sleepily leaning her head against his shoulder. "I'm always causing trouble. Mother and Dad can never decide what to do with me. I'm a terrible example to Hazel."

"So that's your big secret," he said with a soft laugh, and she had to smile.

"What makes you think I've got one?" she asked, looking up into his dark eyes. They were completely soft and open. Understanding. And that was the moment she realized that Donald Jones knew her better than anybody ever had. Because not only did he know, but he *understood*. If the evidence hadn't been right in front of her, she wouldn't have believed it.

"Everybody does," he responded. "We've talked about this before. It's just that since being in Newport, the one thing I've noticed most about everybody here is the secrets you all keep. It's almost as if it's a requirement to be a part of things. Everybody has to have a dark secret or tilted past that nobody talks about. High society is fueled on them." She certainly couldn't disagree with that. But she also wouldn't have been surprised if he'd known every secret hidden behind the mansion walls and crystal chandeliers.

Despite her valiant attempts to hide it, she had to stifle a yawn then, and he sighed, "All right, all right. I'll actually take you home now. Come on." She quickly folded the blanket and hid it back in her car, and followed him to the workbench where he had replaced the kerosene lamp.

But even as the air around them went dark, Rosemary couldn't help wrapping her arms around him in a hug, her left ear once again pressed against his heart. If she'd stopped long enough to analyze her actions, she wouldn't have been able to say what was compelling her to do any of the things she did. It was simply what she had to do. The most natural thing in the world.

When she thought he was pulling away, he merely shifted his arms under hers so that she stood on her tiptoes, her arms wrapped around his neck. He buried his face in her hair and caught the very ends of her curls around his fingers. And she felt a change in the air around them. It was a sort of lift in the immediate surroundings, as if thoughts were shifting. She knew what it was.

"Are you going to kiss me?"

"I was thinking about it," he admitted, and she pulled away, stepping slightly back until her feet were firm on the ground. "What do you think?" In a split second, she went from feeling jumbled and shaky, unsure, and a little frightened at this very open exchange, to feeling completely peaceful. That voice of reason rising again.

"You can kiss me."

"Are you sure?"

"Yes." He didn't stop to ask again, but she would look back later at the fact that he had asked and never cease to marvel.

It wasn't a long kiss, but nor was it timid. It was sure. Completely sure. And when it was over, she only hesitated for one second. "Can we try that again?" He laughed but honored her request. The next few kisses were just as sure, and she couldn't decide if her head was swimming more from disbelief or joy. He hugged her again after the third kiss, and she couldn't help but laugh at what she heard next to her ear.

"Why is your heart pounding so fast?" she teased, and he only laughed before finally leading her out of the garage and to the front door of the house. The sky was no longer indigo, but a sort of royal blue. Slowly transitioning to a beautiful morning sky. They paused at the top of the stairs, hands clasped, both exhausted but hating to part. It didn't matter that they'd see one another the next day.

"Okay, just one more kiss, and then I'll go," he said, and Rosemary didn't have time to smile because she was too eager to accept his kiss. She placed her hand on the back of his head as their lips met, and pulled away slowly. But after that, she forced herself to whisper goodnight and rushed inside. She watched him drive away from the window, and then quickly turned away and hurried to her room while shaking her head.

"So *that's* how that feels."

Eighteen

One week later Ophelia threw a party. It was different from her others in that specific people had been invited, rather than anybody being allowed to show up. It was also held much earlier in the day. The whole group of people was spread about Ophelia's home and grounds: some in the pool, some at the tennis courts, some in the game room.

"I just needed one last bash before I make my escape to Italy," she had explained with a wink as she welcomed Rosemary and Donald inside.

"Well, you've been successful," Rosemary answered. "They'll be talking about this for years and everybody will lie and say they were invited." Ophelia lit a cigarette with a smile, waving it around like a wand.

"Enjoy yourselves then," she said, "or at least try to. I can't be sure if anybody's having a good time but we'll all get through it." They watched her walk back through the crowds and laughed.

"I'll find us drinks," Donald offered, squeezing her hand before disappearing into the crowd. "Where will you be?"

"The game room," she called back, already on her way. As she had suspected, it proved to be the safest bet. There weren't many people there, and the room was a bit darker and cooler.

"Rosemary!" It was Annie Bernard, calling from a card table across the room. Rosemary couldn't remember seeing much of her since very early in the season. Annie had never been the hip type, which was one of the reasons they'd always been able to talk. But now her timid blonde hair had been dyed a rich brown and her lips were painted cherry red. She blew smoke into the air and gestured for Rosemary to join them.

"Hello, Annie," she said, taking the offered chair and smiling at the others seated around the table.

"You'll join our game won't you, Miss Covington?" Howard Thompson said this, a strange smile on his face as he dealt her a hand. Rosemary had never liked him.

"Of course." She was trying hard to smile and blend in, but her heart was beginning to pound profusely and she suddenly felt very anxious. Even in this partially populated room, there seemed to be too many people, too much smoke, too many eyes. There was nowhere to hide, especially from the fear that began clawing at her stomach. Distant music began ringing loudly in her ears. Any moment, she thought somebody might offer her a double scotch and she'd accept it. And then another one. And another.

Rosemary heard Annie's high laugh through the haze and distantly wondered what had happened to her. She wasn't happy. She was miserable, and maybe she even knew that Rosemary could tell that. But try as she might, Rosemary couldn't distract herself with those thoughts. The more time that ticked by, the louder everything got, and the more it seemed that everybody was pressing down upon her. Too much. It was too much like all of that had been. *Where are you, Donald?*

"Oh, there you are." He was suddenly right by her side, the only thing she could see clearly. One look at her and he knew instantly. "Ophelia was looking for you. I guess she needs your help with something." It was a good lie, and his friendliness and laughter covered up any strange behavior on her part as he led her out of the room. He didn't stop until they found an empty room near the back of the house. It had been Rachel's favorite room, and as such, it was rarely used now. But Donald had known that she needed to be alone. And he knew exactly where to take her.

He closed the door firmly behind them and locked it, leading her to a nearby sofa bathed in the afternoon sunlight. The moment he pulled her close, she felt it: safety. She sighed deeply with that feeling as he took her hands and began smoothing them out gently. She hadn't even realized how tightly clenched they had been.

"What is it?" His voice was low and calm, "What happened?"

"Can we just go?"

"No," he shook his head softly, "I don't think we should. Tell me how you're feeling right now. What did they say?"

"Oh, nothing really. It feels stupid now. I'm sorry." She tried to push him away, suddenly embarrassed, but he only pulled her against his chest and leaned them both back on the sofa.

"It isn't stupid," he said then, stroking her hair with his right hand. "I think I understand what happened." Although she felt much calmer, she couldn't hide the fact that she was still shaking. He continued stroking her hair.

"Tell me about London," he requested, "or Frank Sinatra. Tell me anything you want." He was trying to calm her down, and it was so sweet, it made her heart ache.

"London is beautiful," she began, closing her eyes and focusing on his heartbeat. It was quickly becoming her favorite sound. Maybe if she listened to it long enough, her own heart would calm and the prospect of going out into that crowd again wouldn't terrify her. "My favorite place to visit there is Westminster Abbey. I always light a candle and say a few prayers. It really is just so incredible. There is so much history surrounding you and it's fascinating. You can feel it in the air."

"I believe you."

"Frank was born in Hoboken, New Jersey. He really had to fight his way to the top. I firmly believe that there's nothing he can't do," Rosemary smiled. "If you were to ask me my favorite song, I'd have to say *One for My Baby*, even though realistically there are too many to choose from. But that one is beautiful. Even though it's actually quite sad."

"We need to work on your tendency to like tragic things just because you think they're beautiful," he teased, and she laughed. "But go on. What's this song about?"

"A man who has just had his heart broken. He's so in love with some woman, and he's telling a bartender all about it. He's having a drink and singing about his lost love."

"Is he going to go get her back?"

"The song doesn't make it seem that way," she answered. "It ends with him saying that the road before him is very long. Like it would seem after losing the love of your life." She said it so matter-of-factly that he laughed and shook his head.

"Well, then he's a fool. He should run after her. That's not something that you just let go." His voice softened, "Are you feeling any better?"

"Yes," she answered, realizing his distraction technique had worked. "I'm sorry about all of this."

"Don't apologize again," he said in a falsely strict voice, holding her tighter, "it's okay. If you really want to go, we can."

"No, you're right. We should stay. Ophelia is so invested in her last big party. I just got overwhelmed," she sighed. "I'll be okay in a few minutes, and then I'll go out there and put on the best show of wanting to be around these people that you've ever seen." That made him laugh.

"I don't doubt it. Do you want me to leave you alone for a few minutes?"

"No!" She wrapped her arm tightly around his chest and buried her face in his shirt. "Just stay right here with me, please."

"All right," his voice was soothing as he hooked a finger under her chin and lifted her face toward his for a soft kiss, "I'm not going anywhere."

The season was slipping away more quickly than any of them had realized, and with that came many implications. One morning, however, Rosemary realized that there was only one implication that she truly cared about. This recognition occurred only a few days later, near lunchtime on the beach. She and Donald were walking hand in hand, watching Hazel and a few of her friends ride their horses near the water.

"She's talented, isn't she?" Donald asked, gesturing toward Hazel. "She seems more committed to it than her friends."

"You're right," Rosemary answered, tucking her free hand in the pocket of her white pants. "It isn't just something she does for fun like they do. She is very passionate. I keep telling my parents to help her get further into it, whatever that would mean."

"Will they?"

"I think so. Maybe if they could get me out of the way, they could focus on her."

"You don't believe that," Donald said, his voice sure. "Your parents love you a lot. And Hazel, too. They seem different than others I've met here."

"That's because they are," she answered with a smile. "They are much too good for the world at large."

"You say that about a lot of people. And things."

"That's because, underneath my prickly exterior, I prefer to believe in the better side of people. And things."

"Oh, I know." The tone in his voice was nonchalant, as though he'd known this about her since the moment they'd met. Which he probably had.

Rosemary was beginning to understand that this was the way it worked with Donald: they spent time together and had a thousand conversations, and underneath all of it, they were silently absorbing everything there was to know about one another. It was strange that it had happened so quickly. And yet it hadn't stopped feeling like the most natural thing in the world.

"Tell me about your family," Rosemary requested, more than a little fascinated by what it was that had created this person beside her.

"My parents are a lot like yours in that they are much too good for the world." He said this without hesitation. "You know those pictures of suburbs in the catalogs?"

"You mean the ones that always include a skateboard and a dog and rows of perfect little houses?" she asked. "I was always intrigued by those."

"Yes," he laughed, "that's exactly where I grew up. And a lot of how I grew up, actually. But I could never complain about it."

Donald spoke of his childhood with a fondness that caused a strange ache in her heart. An ache to know more, to see it for herself. He continued speaking about his parents, and how he admired their relationship. He became even more enthused when he began speaking about his siblings. Robert and Dawn were older than him, and Alice was younger. Robert had chosen not to join the family in accounting and had gone into medicine instead.

"You worry about living up to him." It wasn't a question. Rosemary knew it was true. He merely shrugged, obviously uncomfortable that the tables had turned between them. She knew him just as well as he knew her.

"Dawn is the kindest person I know. She and I are very close, but if we're together too much, we start to disagree. Typical siblings, I guess. Then there's Alice," he laughed a little, as though there was all at once too much to say about his younger sister and not enough.

"Oh, tell me everything."

"She's very independent and modern," he began. "She is about to begin her last year of high school."

"What then?"

"World domination." He said it casually, but there was a tone of confidence in his voice.

It was clear he had very caring feelings for his younger sister. Perhaps he didn't fully understand her, but it was obvious he believed she could do anything. Even take over the world. Rosemary looked up at him with a smile, and in doing so, felt the world stop for a moment.

Falling in love with Donald Jones was the easiest thing that Rosemary ever did. It had taken no effort. No convincing. It simply was, as if the fact had existed long before either of them and they had finally found it. Looking up at him then, with the full knowledge of everything he was to her, the world began turning again in a new light. And it was so intense that for just a moment, she couldn't breathe.

"Rosemary," Ophelia had a gin in her hand and her reading glasses on the tip of her nose, "you are quite honestly the only one who didn't know that."

Rosemary had just returned from lunch with Donald and Hazel, at a small place near the water. Hazel had continued on with her friends, and Rosemary and Donald had driven back to Ophelia's together. He went back to the guest's cottage to work, and as soon as he was out of sight, she ran as quickly as she could into the main house. Ophelia was perched on the divan in her room, a book in her hand and Ralph nestled in her lap.

"I'm in love with Donald!" she had cried upon bursting into the room. And then Ophelia's response. Upon hearing it, Rosemary fell theatrically onto the bed, which just happened to be the nearest piece of furniture. "What do I do now?"

"First of all, you could stop being so dramatic. Second of all, take a few deep breaths and try to calm down. Do you want a scotch? I'll get you a scotch. We won't tell a soul." Rosemary was severely tempted at the offer. She was on the verge of saying a shifty yes, but then Ophelia set her drink and book down and flopped beside her on the bed. "I obviously have to know everything. What was it that finally made you realize that you are perfect for each other?"

"We were walking on the beach, watching Hazel ride. He was telling me about his family and started talking about his younger sister and how much he cared about her and all the sudden…" Rosemary was too out of breath to finish the sentence just then. "I just knew. It was like running into a wall. And now I'm emotionally compromised."

"It's about time, too," her friend answered. "I was beginning to think it may never happen. Good thing he's the right one."

"What?" Rosemary sat up so quickly that she felt lightheaded. Or perhaps she was lightheaded in general. Both were equally possible at that point. "How can you even say that? How can you know that?"

"It is so obvious that it *hurts,* Rosemary. All of us who see you together know it. It's the most natural thing in the world." Ophelia's eyebrows creased for a moment, "And what's been going on in your head, anyway? You've been spending almost every waking moment with him for weeks.

Did you think you'd just have some kind of fling and then leave him behind and start your real life in London? Because that doesn't sound like you at all. What have you been thinking?"

"I don't know!" Rosemary covered her face with her hands in embarrassment at all the truths being thrown at her. "I didn't let myself think at all about what I may be feeling or where it may be leading! I just went along with it!"

"I'm not sure whether to be impressed that you—of all people—were able to do that, or irritated that it took you this long to see it. In fact, it's taken so long that I was starting to suspect you were just pretending you didn't. Just to make it even more painful for those of us in the audience."

"Oh." It was the only thing Rosemary could think to say as she flopped back onto the soft mattress. "Well, this certainly changes things."

"Understatement of the century, darling. Congratulations."

"But what do I do now?"

"My offer for a secret scotch is longstanding. But in general, I have only one suggestion." It seemed as though Ophelia had had this speech prepared for weeks as she sat up and brought Rosemary with her, looking suddenly very serious. Perhaps she'd even had it prepared for years. "Don't you dare dwell on what you're afraid of, or what you fear could go wrong. This is right. I know you know that. And he knows it, too. Don't sabotage your chance at this much happiness or you'll feel the pain of it forever. And trust me, my dear," she tucked Rosemary's hair behind her ear, "that's a pain you don't leave behind."

"All right." Rosemary's voice caught on unexpected tears in her throat. The type of tears that began burning when you heard transformative truths. "I promise."

"Good." Ophelia's blue eyes suddenly filled with rare tears. "And since you'd rather die than break a promise, I think my work here is done. When will you talk with him about it?"

"Tonight, I guess," she answered, wiping a stray tear and letting out an unsteady breath.

"We're going for a drive after dinner."

Nineteen

When Donald picked her up for dinner that evening, he greeted her with a magnificent smile, wrapping her in a quick hug before leading her back to the car. He looked so handsome, she observed, quickly kissing his cheek when he opened the door for her. His hair was combed in the usual way, a bit messily to the side, and he wore a navy blue shirt with long sleeves. She quickly checked her own appearance in the mirror as he walked around to his seat, but he caught her looking.

"You look beautiful." It was said with the utmost confidence, and he took her hand as he said it. She wished it hadn't made her blush, but she knew that from now on, there would be no hiding her feelings. Part of her wanted to say it right then, shout it even so that all of Newport could hear. *I love you!* But she decided against it. There was too much she needed to say along with it. All of which was best said when he didn't have to focus on driving.

The evening went as they always did. A quick dinner somewhere and then off for a drive, the radio playing as they zoomed along the coast. Rosemary couldn't stop laughing from sheer joy. There were far too many moments with him that she wanted to be painted on her heart, written in her mind forever. So that if she ever needed to, she could retreat inside them and find the safety and happiness there.

They ended up at the beach, a blanket spread beneath them as they watched the waves crash in. The evening air was cool as it brushed onto them over the water. Donald let go of her hand and wrapped an arm around her when he noticed her shivering.

"Do you need a jacket? I have one in the car."

"No." She snuggled her head against his shoulder, "This is perfect." He smiled and pressed a kiss to her forehead, lingering there for a moment. And when he spoke again, his voice was strangely raw.

"Are you really moving to London?" She scrunched her eyes shut in pain at the thought. Because even as he said it, she knew she couldn't. There would be no leaving this behind, no matter how much she loved London. No matter how much other things had called to her in the past. She loved him more than any of that. Rosemary lifted her hand to his face and kissed him.

"No," she finally answered, her breath unsteady and her heart pounding in her ears, "I won't be moving to London."

"Okay." His answer was so simple, yet unmistakably filled with relief, "Good."

"Why?" She knew it wasn't fair to ask, but even though she thought she'd burst with the words, she had to hear them from him first. Donald with his genuine heart and tendency to run. And his frequent inability to decide exactly what his emotions were: she had to know without a doubt that the solid certainty she'd felt from him was *really* there.

He surprised her by smiling, obviously aware of what she was doing, and cupped her chin with his thumb and forefinger. "Because I love you." Her hand was pressed against his chest, and she could feel the pounding of his heart.

"And I love you." The smiles that beamed across both of their faces couldn't have been explained as anything less than childish amazement. Rosemary didn't know whether to kiss him or hug him, but he decided for her when he took her face gently in his hands and kissed her until there were no more words left in her head.

"Wow." It was the first word that dared reenter her mind, and it made him laugh out loud before he pulled her close for a simple hug. Other thoughts slowly began trickling back in as they once again looked out toward the waves.

After some time, he turned to her again and kissed her hair. "I need to tell you something, Rosemary."

"All right. What about?"

"Secrets," he answered with a nervous laugh. "We all have them. And it's time I told you mine." Rosemary was a bit surprised, but nodded, turning to him more fully.

"Okay. I'm ready." He smiled at that and took both of her hands, turning them over and over in his for quite some time before letting out a long breath.

"I run." His words were incredibly simple, but their weight, and everything they implied, sank into her heavily. He suddenly seemed very far away, despite the fact that he was right next to her, their hands intertwined. It was almost enough to frighten her—how suddenly she almost couldn't feel him for a moment. But she didn't say anything. She waited for him to continue.

"I've never been able to just...*live*. Every time I get close, I run away. I push it all away and run as fast as I can in the other direction." Finally, he brought his eyes back to hers, and even though his words should have caused her uneasiness, she felt nothing but surety there. "I get scared, I guess. Or I just don't believe happiness could happen to me. Or other reasons, too, maybe. I'm not exactly sure. So I sabotage it by running away."

"And now?" It was several long seconds before Rosemary could finally ask this, and her words were slightly choked with fear. But he smiled so vividly, then it felt like a bath of sunshine.

"I've never felt anything this real before. I've never been this sure before." She sank into his arms with a grateful laugh and could've cried in joy when the sanctuary of his embrace closed around her.

"So no running?"

He pressed a kiss to her forehead, "No running. Not ever." She couldn't stop smiling and couldn't let go of him. For several long minutes, they sat like this. Both of them unwilling to leave the moment. Several thoughts were drifting in and out of Rosemary's mind as the seconds ticked by. But one thought in particular rose from somewhere deep inside of her, where it had been locked away for years. And scared her more than she'd expected it to.

But the maze of walls inside of her was gone. Donald had removed it brick by brick and replaced it with a large green field where the sun could finally shine. But there was one more thing that had to be done if it was going to remain this way. Any leftover debris had to be cleared. She took a shaky breath.

"What's going on?" He had sensed the shift in the air, the change in her thoughts. Just as she could do with him. She always seemed to be able to reach out with her soul and touch his, but the roles were reversed now.

"Donald, I…" she pulled away from his embrace and turned to face him fully, hating that her lip was already trembling. "I need to tell you my secret, too."

"Rosemary, if you aren't ready—" the concern in his eyes was palpable, but she interrupted him.

"It isn't something you're ever ready for," she said, "but you need to know. I have to know that you know. And that it doesn't change anything."

"It won't change anything," he promised, stroking her hair and then taking both of her hands. "You don't have to tell me everything. Just what you're comfortable with."

But she did tell him everything. She had to.

"It began with a party at Radcliffe. And broken promises."

"You must promise to make me behave myself," Rosemary had said, throwing a double scotch behind her dark red lips as they left the house. "At least more than usual." Everyone had laughed as they piled into the car, the leather seats slick with luxury.

"Nobody holds liquor like you, Rosemary." One of them pointed out, "You'll be the one getting all of us home." She had to laugh in agreement because it wasn't an uncommon occurrence. She reached into the suit coat of the friend sitting next to her, pulling out his golden cigarette case.

"Do you have a light?"

"For you? Always," he chuckled in return, pulling the lighter out and watching her blow the smoke lazily away. She knew what the look in his eyes meant, but she had seen it from many men just like him and was an expert at avoiding it. Acquaintances floated in and out of her life in the usual way, all of them with some idea or another about her. Most of them were wrong, of course, like the ideas reflected in his eyes.

They arrived at the first party of the evening and piled out of the car, many of them linking arms and laughing as they entered the stately home. They all made plans to meet back at the car at some time or another, for there were parties all over town that night. Perhaps Rosemary should have known that she wouldn't be joining them.

She had woken up on the floor in the middle of scattered books. A copy of *Daisy Miller* greeted her mockingly when her eyes fluttered open in the closed light.

She was alone in the room. The lamp had been knocked from the table and glass stuck in the carpets. At first, she wasn't sure if it had cut her. At first, she wasn't sure of anything. There was a pounding in the front of her head, and as the seconds on the grandfather clock in the corner knocked into her ears, she slowly began to feel the ache and pain on every inch of her skin. She tried to move then, but couldn't. And what was more, she couldn't remember why.

Her last lucid memory was drinking a double scotch at the bar the night before. How long into the party had that been? Where had her friends been? Where were they now?

But her head was throbbing too hard to sort out anything. For what felt like forever, she succumbed to the reality that she'd be on the floor until she died.

Eventually, the door of the library opened, and fractured light fell next to her from the opening. Her heart began hammering in her chest, her fists clenched tightly in a reaction to something she couldn't name. Hot water seared her eyes. But she couldn't move, let alone run. It was as though her body was the only thing that remembered exactly what had happened. It was the only one who could react. And it was afraid. Who would be coming through that door?

It was a maid with wide, pale eyes. She saw Rosemary and didn't say a word. With surprising strength, she helped Rosemary off the floor and put her arm around her, leading her to the nearest bathroom. With a scalding cloth, she helped wipe Rosemary clean of glass fragments, blood, and smeared lipstick. And when she was as clean as she could be made, the young woman left her alone for only long enough to call her a cab, and then helped her out to the car.

The cab driver didn't say a word. He didn't ask for payment, either. He drove her home in silence and opened the door for her. He went to offer her his arm to help her to the front door, but her words made decisions for her. They knew things her mind didn't.

"Don't touch me." Her voice was as broken as the glass had been. "Please."

The sunlight was watered down and weak. Its warmth didn't reach her skin. Its light didn't brighten the sky. She finally entered her home and the darkness still left over from the previous night and seemed to realize that she'd never emerge from the darkness again.

Later, she wouldn't be able to remember running the water for a bath or peeling off her dress or where the ruined thing even ended up. She only remembered plunging herself beneath the slightly too hot water. And then scrubbing until her skin was pink and using most of her soap until she realized it would never go away. She'd never be clean again. With this knowledge in her mind, she rose from the water and pulled on a soft, white robe large enough to cover the black bruises. She lay on her bed in the darkness then, a record playing in the background.

This was how Ophelia found her later the same day, her blue eyes iced over in worry. She shouldn't have even been there. They'd had no plans to see each other, yet her friend was suddenly by her side. Ophelia had pushed the still damp hair back from Rosemary's forehead and understood the truth immediately. Rosemary didn't want to say anything, and in fact didn't have to, because Ophelia simply climbed onto the bed next to her and held her in her arms. And together they wept.

Eventually, Ophelia rose and helped Rosemary get dressed. Then she pulled out clothes and a suitcase and drove them away. Though it wasn't the season, they drove to Newport. There would be more privacy there at that time of year. The Covingtons came up from New York the next day, leaving Hazel at home, but Rosemary didn't really remember any of it. That was in fact the deepest problem. And always would be. Everything that she didn't remember.

Rosemary had begun crying too hard to finish. Before she could say the most important thing. But Donald was holding her against him, his arms firmly around her, and not caring that her tears were soaking into his shirt.

"Who was he?" Donald's voice was thick with emotion, but he didn't cry. "What…what *exactly* happened?"

"I'd tell you if I could but…" she burrowed deeper into his embrace, "but I don't remember! That's the problem, Donald, I don't remember! I don't remember because I had too many drinks and I let myself go when I should've been careful! I should've been stronger!"

"No." His voice was strong and not to be argued with. He pulled her away from him and wiped away her tears, his eyes firm. "Don't blame yourself. Please."

"My—" Her words were interrupted by shaky breaths, "Ophelia and Mother made me go to a doctor. They went with me but it was still just so…humiliating. They asked me questions I couldn't answer. Examined me. And then confirmed it. Confirmed everything." She couldn't stand to look into his eyes anymore. They were too full of love, and it hurt. "And ever since then, I've lived in fear. Trying to heal but being unable to. I've been ruled by horrible things that I can't even remember. Wanting the broken pieces to come back together, but not really believing they could."

"And now?" it was simply asked.

"Now?" To her surprise, Rosemary laughed through the tears he had begun wiping away. "Now I believe in all of it. And it's absolutely terrifying." That made him laugh, too.

"Why?"

"Because I don't just want you in my life," she responded, "I...*need* you in my life. And giving that kind of power to somebody…"

"Rosemary." She had to look at him then. "I'm right here." His eyes promised the rest. *I will never hurt you like that. And I'm not going anywhere.* "I love you." Those last words were the biggest promise of all. It had always been far too much to hope for, and yet there it was. Home.

Twenty

Saying goodnight had never been more difficult than it was later that evening. Rosemary quickly lost count of the kisses, or of anything else for that matter. She hadn't thought it possible for absolutely everything to be driven out of her head. It seemed Donald would prove to be the exception in that realm as well.

"All right, I'm just going to count to three and then run inside," Rosemary eventually said. "That's the best way to do this." She only got to two before he kissed her again, and then her resolve was completely gone. She'd have stayed there beside the car with him all night long at that point. Perhaps it was only a few seconds later, or many moments later, but he eventually wrapped her in an embrace. The kind where he buried his face in her hair and toyed with the end of the curls.

"Let's get married," he breathed, and the only thing surprising about it was that it didn't surprise her. It wasn't a proposal, but rather a natural extension of everything. What was it that Ophelia had said? *It's so obvious that it hurts.*

"Okay." Her answer was so simple that he laughed.

"So you'll come back to Cleveland with me?"

"Of course I will," she answered, "but what if your family doesn't like me?"

"Not even a little bit possible." He kissed her again. "They've already heard a lot about you." For some reason, that made her blush and she hid her face in his shirt.

"Well, then you should probably come to dinner with my family or something."

"Or something," he repeated, his voice laced with humor. "What if they don't really like me in a more intimate setting? I've only ever interacted with them at big parties over the season."

"Not even a little bit possible," she teased. "Besides, you're much better at meeting new people than I am. Everybody loves you."

"You can be very charming when you want to be," he countered. "I think it's just a matter of deciding who is worth the effort." She laughed so that he had to hush her, "You'll wake everybody up, and then we'll be in all kinds of trouble."

Rosemary had a few witty things to banter back at him but decided to kiss him instead. He surprised her by pulling away rather quickly as if remembering something important he'd wanted to say.

"What is it?" The crease in his forehead meant it was much more serious than the casual repartee they had perfected.

"I wanted to tell you that I think we should wait until we are married." It was a profound thing to say, and yet his voice was very simple and sure.

"Why?" She wasn't asking because she disagreed, but rather because it was a slight surprise. No matter what traditional values the catalogs printed, reality spoke differently.

"Because you deserve that kind of respect," he said, stroking her hair softly. "And I want to give you the very best. I want to be the very best I can be. Okay?"

"All right."

"Good." The smile returned to his face then, and she could've gotten lost in his eyes. "Then I just require one more kiss and we should try and say goodnight."

Rosemary had heard about happiness her entire life. She had even experienced it in brief spurts: Christmases or achievements, simple summer days. But the concept of living happily, of continuous happiness, was something she'd never found realistic. She knew that people looked for that; for the happiness that was so full, it was all at once damning and saving. Indeed it seemed an elusive destination the whole world was fighting their way toward. And Rosemary had always just assumed that it was a sort of Atlantis. She had assumed everybody would simply die looking for it.

But Donald was an endless well of miracles, teaching her every day that the things she'd long found impossible were not only possible but right before her. They were hers. With every soft kiss or stroke of her hair, Rosemary felt herself going further and further down a path she had long given up on. It was frightening, so much more than she had known, but even in that, there was comfort. It wouldn't be so terrifying if it weren't right.

The season was drawing to its inevitable close. Many of the last big parties were done with, leaving behind plumes of smoke and empty bottles. Most of the big names were leaving Newport, and the houses were being shut up until the next visit. The Covingtons always stayed a bit longer than most, preferring to enjoy the last of the summer still away from the city.

Ophelia's preparations to move to Italy were all but finished. Rosemary spent days in her room with her, looking at photos of the new property and helping her decide on decorations.

"There will be a special guest room solely dedicated for your use," Ophelia had said one day, "so you can't wait too long to visit." All of it was almost more than Rosemary could bear—seeing Ophelia so happy, feeling this happiness herself. She often felt like a small child, her heart so full that she could barely focus on anything.

When Donald wasn't finishing up Ophelia's business, he was with Rosemary. Two weeks before the Covingtons were scheduled to return to New York City, they planned the family dinner with Donald. There would be mashed potatoes, a mountain of them, and a sparkling punch Hazel had insisted on. It had been some weeks since their time on the beach, and as such, their new truths had sunk deep until they were all that existed.

Rosemary drove to the guest cottage early in the afternoon and snuck in the back door. She made her way as quietly as she could to his office, pausing in the doorway to watch him work. When he was concentrating, he bit the tip of his tongue in the right corner of his mouth, and his eyes scrunched a bit behind his glasses. He ran a hand through his hair, pushing it off his forehead. Something whispered to her then that the rest of her life sat before her. Like a wonderful gift that she had been given and couldn't believe it was real. She almost had to leave then, because it was so lovely, it was beginning to ache.

"If your aim is to sneak around, I suggest you don't think honestly about a career in espionage." He turned to her with a laugh, leaving his folders behind to scoop her into his arms. And even on a normal afternoon in a seemingly normal embrace, she felt the safety of his arms tangibly. "I didn't think I'd see you before the party tonight."

"I couldn't possibly wait that long," she answered, burying her face in his shoulder and breathing deeply. He had a nice smell: a combination of clean and just *him*. "It's been at least ten hours since I saw you last."

"All right, but just for a little bit or Ophelia will fire me." His voice wasn't very convincing as he led her down the hall and into the kitchen. "Are you hungry?"

"Do you have a soda?" He laughed at that and grabbed her one from the fridge, but paused before giving it to her, a gentle crease in his forehead.

"I haven't kissed you yet today." She didn't have time to laugh at his seemingly genuine distress; instead, she gave him a quick kiss and stole the soda from his hand.

"I've been on the telephone with my mother today," Donald said, getting himself a soda and coming to stand next to her, both of them leaning against the oven.

"And?"

"She's very excited to meet you. I told her some of the things we've been planning."

"What did she have to say about it all?"

"Only two words: she's perfect." He beamed at her when he said it, wrapping an arm loosely around her shoulders. The very idea seemed too wonderful to be the truth, and yet that seemed to be the reality Rosemary was dealing with now.

"I'm very excited to meet her, too. And Alice. We have so much to discuss about her world domination." He laughed and drained the rest of his drink, pulling her in for a hug.

"I want you to stay but I know that if you do, I won't get any work done."

"Why?" She thought she pulled off the innocent voice rather well and even batted her eyelashes a little. But of course, he knew she was teasing.

"I'll be early for dinner tonight. Meet me in the driveway?"

"You've got a deal," she answered, setting her empty bottle next to his and flashing a smile at him. "I'll see you then."

"Wait, wait, wait." He caught her arm as she was walking away and brought her back toward him.

Rosemary knew that he was pulling her back for one more kiss, but from the instant their lips met, it wasn't like anything they had previously shared. His lips were soft and inviting against hers. She felt his arm push around her back, pulling her as close as he could, his free hand winding into her hair. Her own arms slid around him as he tilted her head back just a bit, enough to press his mouth against hers in a way that was both unfamiliar and intensely necessary.

A deep hunger rose up between them, filling whatever empty spaces were left within the clasp of their embrace. They broke apart only momentarily, their breathing heavy before the intensity pulled them back together again.

Rosemary got lost in these kisses—in his taste and smell and how his back felt under her hands. The way his lips moved against hers urgently as though they shared the same thoughts. And when they finally pulled apart again, Rosemary almost had to physically shake her head to get words back into it.

"I'm going now," her tone indicated that she had to say it out loud so that somebody could be held responsible. "I'll see you tonight." It took every ounce of resolve she could muster, and even a prayer, to extricate herself from his embrace.

"I'll see you tonight." His voice was scratchy, and the air between them was so thick that walking away felt like breaking magnets apart.

Twenty-One

"So the idea of moving to Cleveland doesn't scare you?" Hazel asked her this a few hours later when they were together in Rosemary's room getting ready for dinner.

"Not at all," Rosemary answered, putting a record on and joining her younger sister at the vanity. "I am a little nervous to meet his family. I'm afraid they won't see me the way he does. But I'd go anywhere in the world with him."

"Just as long as you were together?" Hazel sounded teasing when she said it, but she understood nonetheless. She had a habit of being playful about Rosemary's tendency to feel everything so deeply.

"Yes," Rosemary answered with a laugh, holding up several pairs of earrings before she settled on one. "How do you feel about all of this, Hazel? Be honest." As if Hazel needed a reminder to say exactly what she thought.

"Honestly," Hazel began, turning to look at her older sister, "it is strange because it isn't strange. I always thought that when you finally found somebody you felt this way about, it would be odd to see you together, to hear your plans. But it isn't. It just feels normal. Like it's always been this way." She looked back into the mirror briskly, "But I am going to miss you."

"I'll miss you, too." Rosemary couldn't help pulling her in for a firm hug, even though Hazel didn't usually like that sort of thing. She even pressed a kiss to her cheek, which she usually only did to irritate her younger sister. But Hazel didn't seem to mind this time.

"Can I choose your dress for tonight?"

"Please do," Rosemary answered, running a brush through her hair. "You're always better at that than I am."

"Simple, yet elegant," Hazel called from the closet, "I'll find the perfect thing."

"What are you wearing?"

"Something red, I think," her voice was muffled, presumably buried under taffeta and silk. "But I'm not sure yet. I have to make a good impression on Donald, obviously. I don't want him to be ashamed to have me as a sister."

"He'd never think that," Rosemary said it more to herself than to Hazel, since her sister's voice was dripping with good humor. It was clear she could tell what type of person Donald was. He was so genuinely kind and had such a desire to help others. It was hard to miss.

"What is it that you love most about him?" Hazel asked this as she emerged from the closet, holding a tea-length dress with a fitted blacktop. The neck was wide, perfect for a statement necklace, and the skirt was full and cream-colored.

"He is just so…" It was irritating how tears pricked at her eyes. Happiness had turned her so soft. "*Good*," she finished with a nod. "He's so genuinely good. So much better than I'll ever be. He makes me feel as though I have some goodness in me, a gentleness I'd prefer to hide. But he can see me. Really see me."

"And you can see him."

"Yes," Rosemary finished. She was glad her sister seemed to understand as she had no further way of explaining it.

"So tell me what your plans are specifically," Hazel said, laying jewelry and shoes next to the dress. "You're going back to Cleveland with him, but then what? Are you formally engaged now? Where will you get married? When will you get married? And will you work there? He can't honestly expect you of all people to be an ordinary housewife."

Rosemary laughed, "I think that what we have now is a formal understanding. He doesn't want to officially propose until I've met his family."

"Understandable."

"We've talked a little bit about when we'll be married, but mostly where. There's a beautiful church in Cleveland he has told me about. As far as me working, I'll start looking around at newspapers the second we get there. Though he's always telling me he wants me to start working on a novel at some point." She turned to her younger sister then, suddenly quite serious, "Will you be my maid of honor?"

"I'd love to," Hazel said, lifting her hand as though raising a glass, "to the future Mrs. Jones."

Dinner went better than Rosemary could've hoped. She had been worried that it would be tense and awkward, with all of them suddenly forced to interact for a more meaningful purpose than a casual meeting. But instead, it felt calm and natural. Perfect, even.

With the meal behind them, they retreated into a nearby room for coffee, though Hazel skipped past them all and put a record on the turntable. The music was jazzy and fun, spilling out of the room and into the marble-tiled entryway. It filled the entire house, as did so many other things that evening.

Donald suddenly set his coffee cup down and took Hazel by the hand, shouting over the music, "Come dance with me!" Rosemary's laugh matched her younger sister's as she watched them fly out into the entryway where there was more room. They began a playful swing dance, and Hazel couldn't have hidden her blush if she tried, but she was happy. Arthur and June soon joined them. Rosemary followed to stand in the doorway, leaning against the polished wood and drinking her coffee as she watched the spectacle before her. She thought it was the most beautiful thing she'd ever seen.

When the second song began, Hazel and Donald kept dancing, as though they were just warming up. June and Arthur left with a laugh, joining Rosemary at the door.

"What do you think, Rosemary?" It had always been her father's way of asking how she felt about life in general. But the smile that split across her face was all the answer he needed.

"He's wonderful, dear, just so wonderful," June said, tears filling her green eyes. "I'll have to thank him later."

"For what?"

"For everything," June said, kissing her cheek. "And tell him he's more than welcome in the family. He belongs here.

I felt it the moment you walked in together." June left to retrieve her coffee, but Arthur smiled and took Rosemary's hand.

"Come dance with me, sweetheart. We'll see if they can take the heat." They all lost track of time as they danced the evening away—switching partners around and changing records when one finished. Eventually spent with playful dances, Arthur put on *Frankly Sentimental* and winked at Rosemary when the soft music began filling each corner of the house. Donald grinned at Rosemary but begged for a break, leaving her to dance with Hazel.

"We've got to stop meeting like this," Hazel teased as they swayed to the soft lyrics of *Body and Soul*. "What will people say?"

"That we're creating all kinds of scandals," Rosemary teased back, and then grew a bit more serious. "So...what do you think?"

Hazel surprised her by laughing and shaking her head in dismay. "He's perfect, Rosemary. Absolutely perfect. I'm happy for you." It was so rare for her sister to show such depth in her emotions that Rosemary had to fend off tears.

"Please don't get all sappy on me," Hazel teased, whipping Rosemary out in a dramatic twirl that didn't fit the song at all. "When it's right, it's right. It doesn't have to be dramatic. Just be grateful and move forward with it. Let yourself be happy. It's really simple." Hazel finished out the song they were now on and left Rosemary in Donald's waiting arms before skipping over to Arthur and June.

"What?" Donald asked with a smile, pulling her in close as *One for My Baby* began playing.

"Someday I hope to be half as wise as my younger sister," Rosemary answered, and then tilted her head when she realized what song was playing. "This is it! This is it! Okay, just listen." He laughed a little and shook his head, pulling her just a little closer as they fell into the rhythm of the song.

"I still think he's an idiot," he whispered near her ear a ways into the song. "If he loves her this much, why is he letting her go?"

"I don't know," she answered, settling her head on his shoulder. "It's so sad. He'll just have his drink and leave, and try and live life without her. The song calls their time together a 'brief episode' but the length obviously didn't matter. His heart is completely broken."

"He needs to put his drink down and get her back," he smiled. "But now I'm passionately discussing Frank Sinatra lyrics and I'm not sure what that means."

"It means you've come so far," Rosemary laughed, looking up into his full eyes. "I'm so proud of you." If it was possible, his eyes seemed to soften further and he bent to kiss the tip of her nose.

"I love you."

Twenty-Two

They ended the family evening fairly early, and Rosemary practically had to pry Donald away from the embraces and handshakes. Though it was much too early in the evening to even entertain the notion of saying goodnight to one another.

"Where should we go?" Donald asked as they drove away, Rosemary snuggling close to him on the seat. They decided on the beach, but first Rosemary insisted on stopping by Ophelia's. Her friend would want to know how the family evening had gone. They separated at the back door, Rosemary to go tell Ophelia everything as quickly as it could be managed and Donald to the guest house for some blankets. It would be chilly by the water.

Rosemary walked inside, finding the house strangely empty. Not even Anthony to welcome her in. "Ophelia?" she called, her voice echoing oddly off the marble. She'd have thought her friend was perhaps gone if all the lights hadn't still been illuminating every corner. "Ophelia?" She walked further into the house and finally heard music, drifting downstairs from Ophelia's rooms. No wonder she hadn't heard her.

"Ophelia! I have so much to tell you!" Rosemary shouted, rushing up the stairs and toward the tall bedroom doors. "You were right! Everything is..." Rosemary opened the door just before she finished this sentence, and stopped in her tracks. "Perfect." It came out in a choked whisper.

It wasn't her moment to see. It wasn't her secret to know. So much so that when she saw it there, before her eyes, she almost didn't believe it. And it was all black and white. Black lace clinging to Ophelia's white skin, a starched shirt open to reveal a black chest. Anthony hadn't been at the door to welcome Rosemary inside because he was here with Ophelia. Their arms were wrapped around one another as they shared a kiss that was both deeply passionate and intensely familiar. And for the merest of seconds, Rosemary thought that if she silently closed the door and ran away, that none of it would be true. That perhaps she could return to a world where her best friend didn't keep secrets like this.

But it was too late for that.

"Rosemary!" Ophelia called after her as she turned and fled. But her vision was blurry, her head was spinning, and it didn't take long for Ophelia to catch up to her on the staircase. "Rosemary, I'm so sorry! You weren't supposed to—I thought you were with—that wasn't—"

"How long?" It took a great amount of effort to even get those words out. Rosemary slid down and sat on the steps, and the marble was a shocking cold against her legs. Like betrayal.

"A few years," Ophelia's voice was raspy as she sat next to her. The beautiful lace she wore looked wilted now. "I...I wanted to tell you, Rosemary. Oh, I so wanted to tell you but—"

"But what?" Of all the emotions Rosemary felt, it seemed that anger was the first to win the battle for expression. "But what, Ophelia? You couldn't trust me to keep your secret? Me of all people? You couldn't trust *me*?" She clenched her fists and stood, unable to sit next to her friend. No matter the tears that were running out of the open blue eyes.

"Rosemary..." Anthony appeared at the top of the stairs then, approaching Ophelia with gentle concern. A very thick veil had been lifted, and Rosemary couldn't believe she hadn't seen it sooner. "Ophelia did want to tell you. She's always wanted to tell you. But the consequences of something like this getting out..." There were consequences. Past how dreadful the scandal itself would be, there were legal consequences in many states.

"If you think this about the color of your skin, Anthony, you don't know me at all," Rosemary said, not even trying to keep the venom from her words.

"Well, the rest of the country doesn't see it that way!" Ophelia shouted, jerking away from Anthony's comforting touch and approaching her friend. "Do you have any idea how terrible it would be for both of us if something like this got out? I didn't want to keep this from you! Don't you think I've thought about how much it would hurt you when you eventually found out? That all the years you've been broken and trying to heal and letting me see your secrets would only get worse when you realized I couldn't let you see mine? I know all of that!"

"This is the real reason you're moving." Rosemary didn't even recognize her own voice. "So the two of you can finally get married and live together in peace. Because you'd never be able to do that here." There was a chill in the air with the speaking of those truths. "And you had your work brought to you this summer so that you wouldn't have to be apart while you planned everything." A very deep sigh left her then. As though she'd been holding her breath for hours. She turned to leave, but Ophelia stopped her.

"Please don't leave like this," she begged. "You are my dearest friend. My sister. I never wanted to hurt you like this. I want to share it with you. But I couldn't."

"I just…want to be happy for you. With you," Rosemary answered, not realizing that she had tears running down her own face. "And now I find out that you've been keeping the biggest part of your life a secret from me for years. *Years*!" There was a strange silence in the house after Rosemary said this. Strange because the hurt didn't come from disapproval or malice. It only came because happiness had been kept hidden when it shouldn't have been something to be ashamed of.

She looked at the two of them, standing side by side, and realized even in her moment of hurt how well they fit together. How happy they both were. And hated that it didn't matter, hated that the pain of betrayal caused her tears to burn hot. Hated that of all people, Ophelia stood before her and seemed like a stranger. She turned and left.

It was dark enough outside that Donald didn't see the tear streaks on her face as she approached the car. He only saw the silhouette of the woman he loved approaching him, and he could've burst with pride at the thought.

He grinned and called to her, "I knew it would take longer to tell her everything. What did she have to say?" Rosemary ignored his words, suddenly rushing into his arms where the tears began again. But it didn't matter then. Not with his arms holding her tightly against the beat of his heart. There was always a promise of complete safety there.

"What happened?" His voice was a mixture of shock and concern. "Are you all right? What's going on?"

"You were right about everybody having secrets, Donald." She hugged him even tighter, and her tears were spreading makeup all over his starched white shirt.

"What do you mean?" His voice sounded soft against her harsh sobs, but she was crying too hard to truly explain anything. He stroked her hair softly and pressed a kiss to her forehead, content to wait until she could say more.

"Ophelia…Ophelia and Anthony…I saw them…"

"Oh." The sudden understanding in his voice was unmistakable. "I know."

"What?" She jerked out of his embrace roughly, mopping her tears away to try and read his eyes. "What do you mean, you know?"

"I've worked with Ophelia in her home for months, Rosemary," he explained. "It didn't take long for me to put the pieces together. I've known almost since the beginning."

"And you didn't think it was a good idea to tell me?" He couldn't have missed the anger and hurt in her voice that was quickly turning in his direction.

"At first, I just assumed that you knew." His voice was infuriatingly calm, trying to soothe her. Not wanting to be the object of her anger, and hating that he'd contributed to the hurt. "But then once I realized you didn't, I knew that I couldn't say anything. It wasn't my secret to tell. Do you think I wanted to get between Rosemary Covington and Ophelia Baxter? Would you?"

"I don't know what I would have done!" He tried to take her hands but she stepped away. "I don't know anything! Everyone asks to see every inch of my secrets, to look at every corner of my darkness. But at the end of the day, *I'm* apparently the one who can't be trusted. Was she just going to move to Italy, marry Anthony, and never tell me?"

"It had nothing to do with you being trustworthy, Rosemary." His voice was so gentle, and his eyes were so pleading that she couldn't push him away this time. "It must have killed her every day that she couldn't tell you. But to protect them both, they couldn't tell anybody. Not anybody. She loves him and he loves her. And in the end, that is what you have to protect above all else. That's all that matters."

Twenty-Three

For several days, Ophelia's house seemed to be a foreign world to her. A world she did not understand and was therefore not welcome in. It was ridiculous, she knew, because Ophelia was certainly waiting for her return. But Rosemary couldn't bring herself to go for much longer than she would've thought.

Donald only spoke of it when she did, and never pressed her. There was a gentle knowing in his dark eyes that said she'd come to understand it. And though it irritated her, she knew he was right. In the meantime, they had long talks about simple nothings. They sat in the car under a field of stars, or on the beach in the sand. He made her laugh and interrupted her with kisses and very slowly helped her remember what was truly important.

And so eventually, she did make her way back to the large white house. Anthony let her back inside with the most genuine smile she'd ever seen him wear. He knew she was only back now because she was ready.

Ophelia was in her office with Donald, both of them looking rather bookish as Rosemary walked into their sea of charts and jargon. And as they both saw her enter, for a moment she couldn't tell which of them looked happier.

Donald positively beamed with pride as he gathered his things up and left them alone, stopping to hug her quickly and kiss her cheek. His eyes twinkled down at her as he left the room.

Rosemary turned from him and met Ophelia's eyes across the room. Her friend's serene smile and mint green dress began to blur in the wake of Rosemary's tears. It seemed that they stood looking at one another for a long time, though it was only a few seconds. And then Ophelia said something that was completely unexpected.

"Do you think they would be proud of me?"

"You're happy." These were the words Rosemary said, but they meant *of course*. Ophelia all but crumpled into her arms then. Her green dress made her look so innocent. As if the little girl who had lost her parents had finally realized that she was whole again. It wasn't like Ophelia to let her heart leak through her skin so much, but it was a moment when she let Rosemary see everything she'd ever hidden. Her soul laid bare.

When they finally pulled apart, Rosemary dabbed the tears from off her friend's face and let her out to the verandah, where a pitcher of iced tea waited in the sun, and a Frank Sinatra record greeted their newness. Very slowly, they began to talk again. They spoke of both of their plans: Rome and Cleveland. Weddings. Children and careers. Futures brighter than the sunlight surrounding them. Promises of happiness sealed in mint green.

"Will you come to help me pack in a few days?" Ophelia asked later as Rosemary walked out of the door. "I'll need help deciding what to take right away and what to have sent later."

"Absolutely. If you'll come to help me do the same thing."

"It's a deal," Ophelia promised, and Rosemary grinned at that as she made her way over to the guest house, finding Donald in his office. His desk was covered in papers and his eyes looked blurry. But his smile when he saw her was enough to clear away anything. She accepted his gentle embrace and felt her heart swell when he kissed the top of her head.

"I'm proud of you," he said, briefly brushing her cheekbone with his thumb. "Why don't we go somewhere to celebrate?"

"Come into the kitchen with me and I'll make you something," Rosemary said, pulling him down the hall. "Won't that be fun?"

"You cook?" He was obviously teasing, but she pretended to be angry as she fished an apron out of a drawer.

"As a matter of fact, I'm an amazing cook, Mr. Jones. You'll see. I'll make an exemplary housewife."

"Please don't," he said, pulling her close to stroke her hair. It seemed he could never believe how soft it was. "You and I are not and never will be a catalog couple. I want you to be an exemplary you. That's who I fell in love with." He kissed her once, then twice.

"I'm trying to cook." It was a weak complaint at best, and he didn't seem to care. He took the apron that was still in her hand and tossed it behind her, where it landed in the sink.

"I like this idea better." Rosemary smiled at his playfulness and eagerly accepted his next several kisses, laughing when he led her out of the kitchen and toward the sofa in the library. He did it with a mischievous smile that suddenly made her terribly shy. Even blush. He chuckled when he saw it, pulling her close to him on the sofa.

"Don't be shy," he murmured into her hair, "I just want to kiss you." And when he did kiss her again, it was very soft and sweet, as though he was afraid she might break. As if he was trying to protect her. He often kissed her like that.

After several moments, Rosemary pulled away, leaning her head against the soft cushion, her face still inches from his. She reached up timidly to stroke his cheek, which was a bit rough with stubble. To his surprise, she carefully took his glasses off and set them on a nearby table, so she could more easily see into his eyes. They held a smile. Happiness. The silence between them wasn't strained as Rosemary brushed her thumb over his cheekbone, suddenly fascinated with every aspect of his face.

"Rosemary?"

"Hmm?" She moved her eyes back to meet his and saw an unbelievable tenderness there that she could barely stand.

"If any of this ever scares you, or brings up painful memories or anything like that, will you tell me?" For a moment, she could only nod because it was so sweet, it nearly broke her heart.

"Yes," she finally whispered back, "though I don't think that's something to be worried about. I used to worry about it all the time. But not with you." She tilted her head just a bit further toward his, "I'm always safe with you." When she looked into his eyes at that moment, she almost gasped at what she saw there. It was her. As if he'd accepted her fully and made her a part of him. And she suddenly understood why Jay Gatsby had wanted Daisy back at all costs. She understood why people preached about and died for love. It was more real than anything. He smiled because he knew.

"I love you."

Donald pulled her into a kiss that was overwhelming in its tenderness and simplicity. As if to seal everything that had been said and unsaid. When they pulled away from that kiss, their eyes met in a single moment of connection. And then he was kissing her again, with a hunger that welled up from deep inside both of them. As if to make certain that they each knew what bound them together so tightly.

The same passion that had risen between them days before in the kitchen was suddenly there again, but somehow more pressing. One silent thought hung in the air: *I am yours and you are mine.* Everything else was choked out of existence because it wasn't necessary.

In the wake of these truths, Rosemary felt one of his hands snake into her hair and get tangled there, the other one urgently pressing against her waist to bring her closer to him. She was aware of her arms pushing around him, of her hands pressing flat into the contours of his back and there gathering fistfuls of his shirt. Very dimly, Rosemary recalled that a reason for them to stop doing this existed, but with his caresses burning into her skin, that thought quickly fled. There was nothing but him.

The buttons on his shirt came into contact with her fingertips then just as a trail of kisses made their way along her jaw. She heard a noise from down the hall, only realizing it was the telephone after an eternity of trying to figure out what could possibly exist besides them.

"Donald, the telephone." She managed to say the words, but everything else was focused on the next button on his shirt.

"It can wait." His voice was scratchy and low as he kissed her again, breaking their lips apart for only a second with a deep laugh when she easily accepted that statement and buried her fingers in his hair. If the air had been less thick, and his touch less urgent, perhaps she would've laughed with him and the moment might have abated. She might have been able to remember that they had had a discussion about this. And that it was being flagrantly disregarded.

But there had never been any conscious moment of realizing they were close to a cliff and deciding to take the leap. It had simply happened. And now there was only the very crucial need to make certain that there would never be any reason to doubt what had passed between their eyes. The only thing Rosemary remembered consciously thinking was that if he ever stopped, she would die. Everything else that came into her mind was sensation—his fingertips pressed into the center of her back, and her fingers finally working out the last of his buttons before she pushed the loose folds of his shirt out of her way.

When the telephone began ringing again, it may as well have been on a different planet. Rosemary was too far away for anything other than Donald to exist. He heard it faintly, like an echo of a memory that had been important once. And then he became sharply aware of the heat between them, of the depth of their kiss, of every beautiful detail of Rosemary invading his mind completely. And somehow he pulled away. Just far enough to press his forehead against hers and murmur, "I'll go answer it...I'll be right back..."

Rosemary's eyes opened as if it was the first time she'd seen the room—as if she'd been away for a very long time. She held on to him firmly and helped them both sit up. But it hardly helped. Their limbs were still tangled together; his touch was still too hot against her skin. His breath still mingled with her own.

"All right." She said it in the strongest voice she could muster, which was still weak with need. "You just go answer it. You go." She almost had to physically push him away, just to put space between them. He left the room shakily, barely able to remember how to button his shirt back up and tuck it in.

Though his voice was muffled, Rosemary could hear the sounds of a lengthy discussion. She shook her head a bit and brushed her hands together over and over again, as if those actions would clear the sensations still clinging to her skin. But they didn't. She looked down at herself and found several of her own buttons open, which she quickly did up as she left the sofa and the library behind her. She didn't know how long Donald would be on the telephone, but the thought of sitting in that room and waiting for his return was nearly unbearable. She smoothed out the wrinkles in her blouse as she stepped outside into the cool evening air.

The sun was sitting happily in the sky, sinking lower toward the horizon. A stiff breeze blew her curls back from her face as it ran off the ocean. She walked a ways away from the house and sank gratefully into the lush grass. It was a bit damp. But the moisture felt refreshing against her bare feet. She realized that her fists were clenched and looked down at them in surprise. Slowly, she forced her fingers out of the fists and watched the normal color return back to them.

Close was hardly the correct word to describe what had happened. They had been more than close. She wondered at the thoughts that were running through his mind. But when it came to matters of great importance like this, Donald was notoriously wretched at deciding how he felt. Unless it came to his feelings for her. It was the one thing he'd been completely and utterly certain of. But this? She guessed that he might be disappointed. Mostly in himself. He would try to take all the blame.

But would he regret it?

This was the largest question on Rosemary's mind. For she found rather suddenly that she would certainly never regret it. If anything, the experience had been one of hope. Nagging thoughts had always lingered in the corners of her mind, taunting her at the possibility that getting so near to somebody like that would bring her past back in full force. But it hadn't. There had been nothing and nobody but him. Nothing but that desire to make absolutely certain that he knew everything he was to her. And whether or not Rosemary viewed what they had done as right or wrong, the fact remained that they had previously agreed not to even approach such a situation. And yet they had approached it. She shook her head at the thought.

It was several moments before she heard the door of the house close softly, and the rustle of Donald's feet in the grass as he approached. He sat down beside her, bringing his knees up and resting his arms on them. She was sitting similarly and their elbows brushed as he settled in. She smiled just a bit as his presence calmed every tumultuous thought in her head. Even sitting next to him, like this, was a sanctuary.

He looked over at her slowly, and though he didn't try to physically touch her, she felt him reaching out nonetheless.

"Please look at me, Rosemary."

"I don't want to look at you right now." It wasn't what she had expected to say. She felt peace between them, yes, but what else would she see in his eyes?

"I love you." His voice was so soft, it could've shattered against the air. He reached out very slowly and wrapped one of her curls around his finger. When he spoke again, the words were halting and unsteady, "It didn't scare you, did it?"

She turned to him almost incredulously, the words "Is that what you think?" on the tip of her tongue. But what she saw in his eyes so perfectly reflected everything she held in her own that no words came. And she found very suddenly that the only way she could think to respond was to take his face in her hands and kiss him just once. With every bit of sincerity she held.

"Do you regret it?" Only then could she find the strength to ask him.

"Oh, no," he whispered in return, tucking her curls behind her ear. His eyes were so full of emotion that they gleamed. He wasn't crying. Donald never cried. But this was almost like it. "I may be a little surprised. Perhaps disappointed in myself." He shook his head and let his hands fall back to his sides. "We made a promise to each other. And I'm the one who tried to break it."

"There's no point in blaming yourself." She blushed and had to look away. "I was a very willing participant." He laughed at that and pulled her close, right next to the beat of his heart.

"We can't let that happen again." His voice was still serious, but it held a soft edge of lightness now. She nodded her agreement and let silence settle between them. "What are you thinking about?" he asked after several moments.

She smiled and looked up at him, "Just something that Hazel said to me a few weeks ago. At the dinner we had for you."

"Tell me everything."

Rosemary laughed, "She said it to me while we were dancing. She told me you were perfect. And she said that when it is right, it's right. It doesn't have to be complicated. She told me to take my happiness and run."

"Wise advice." He kissed the top of her head. "I do believe we'll listen to it."

"Oh, good," she answered, and then very suddenly asked, "Can we just get married?" She didn't expect him to laugh out loud at this question, but he did, squeezing her in a tight embrace before helping her up.

"Yes." His answer was firm, "Yes, we can."

"I love you." She made sure she looked into his eyes when she said it, and he smiled in return before kissing her lips, and then the tip of her nose.

"You are much too good for me, Rosemary," he grinned, "but it's a burden that I am more than willing to bear. Come on, the diner has a special tonight that we'd be crazy not to take advantage of."

Twenty-Four

Even when Rosemary was not with Donald, there was a connection between them. One that she could physically feel. And if she went too long without seeing him, or even hearing his voice, it was almost as though something inside of her started to wither. She had heard people who were in love talk about this before and had never hesitated to poke fun at them. *Why put so much dependency on another person?* Past Rosemary had often thought. *Why let somebody have that much power over you?*

It seemed now that the universe was bent on proving to Rosemary that she, too, could fall under this spell. And that it was anything but foolish. It was, in fact, incredibly remarkable. The most remarkable thing. She often caught herself mulling over it. Torn between brief moments of not believing it was true and throwing herself at its mercy.

There was a great deal to do in the short time left before they were to leave for Cleveland, and Rosemary was quickly caught up in the preparations. Days later, she found herself in her room, buried in boxes and suitcases. Hazel had long since given up helping her, and Ophelia wouldn't be able to arrive until later. As such, her record player and a pitcher of iced tea seemed to be her only valiant help until an unexpected knock came at her door.

"Come in!" Her voice was most likely muffled through piles of clothing and even more piles of books.

"Good morning!" Donald's voice was jovial as he burst into the room. "I was ordered to come and help because…" his voice trailed off at the scene before him, and Rosemary's head suddenly appeared from behind a pile of dresses.

"Because I've been abandoned by everybody else." She picked her way through the maze until she got to him, giving him a quick kiss. "But I seriously doubt you want to help me make these kinds of decisions. I don't even want to make them. Can't I just take one suitcase of clothes and send the rest away? And then I'll have plenty of room for all my books."

He laughed, but it wasn't his normal laugh. Easily given. He looked shaken, no matter how bravely he was trying to hide it.

"Donald, what's wrong?" A host of feelings suddenly flooded into her mind, feelings that were not her own. They were his.

"This just…" he shook his head. "It's real. It's really going to happen." A feeling of relief washed over her like a tidal wave when he pulled her into his arms. Relief for the safety of his embrace, relief because she knew exactly how he was feeling.

"There are so many unknowns," she admitted. "It is a little frightening at times."

"But?" he prodded.

"But it's right," she answered simply, and he nodded in understanding. "I've never been more certain of anything."

"Me, too." He smiled and kissed her forehead, moving over to the nearest pile of books. "I'll be in charge of this. It seems easy enough. Are there any you want to take right now or are you packing all these up?"

"I've already sorted out the books I'm taking now. You can pack all of those up in that trunk. In alphabetical order and by genre, please."

"You're joking," he looked at her in disbelief and she laughed.

"Yes, I am. Pack them in however they'll fit best." Donald couldn't stay long. He had packing of his own to do and Ophelia's last-minute business to tie up. They were so close to the future, they could almost reach out and touch it.

"Wait just a minute!" Donald said a few moments later, his voice falsely upset as he picked up a copy of *Les Misérables*. "Why isn't this in the 'take immediately' pile? I demand a reasonable explanation." Rosemary suddenly remembered that she had once told him she'd read it, a half-truth she'd forgotten to correct.

"I'll hardly need it in the few weeks it will take for the rest of this to catch up with us," she explained lightly, which made him smile. Reluctantly, he put it inside the trunk and shut the lid, standing to leave.

"I just love *Les Misérables* so much," he said, pulling her in for a hug. "And you, of course."

"Of course." She laughed at his teasing and accepted a kiss. And then several more. "Will I see you tonight?"

"We'll see how far I get with business. I'm trying to get it all finished up either today or tomorrow so that I can focus on other things," he answered, pressing his forehead to hers. "But if not tonight then in the morning. We'll talk soon."

"Promise?" For reasons she couldn't explain, Rosemary suddenly needed his reassurance. She needed to be able to reach out and feel his surety as she had always been able to. It wasn't a promise that they would talk soon that she needed. It was the other promises he'd always been so sure about giving. If she could feel that surety one more time before they left, it would be all that was needed to make her strong enough for the unknowns. He looked into her eyes and smiled, as though he knew exactly what she was thinking.

"I promise."

Rosemary spent most of the next day with Ophelia, and her packing was much more extensive. There was no telling when her friend may come back to the United States for any extended stay. And as such, there was a great deal of planning involved. She would always keep her Newport residence and her plantation, of course, but she told Rosemary of how the sale of her New York residence was finalizing.

"Luckily I finished most of that before we came up for the season," Ophelia said. They were currently in the library, sticking papers with instructions on the shelves. "But the problem is that I still want to leave some of my things here. I just can't stand the thought of this house being empty and alone." Rosemary understood that well enough. There were so many pleasant memories from Ophelia's childhood in this home.

"I understand," she said, glancing out the window toward the guest cottage. "Have you spoken with Donald this morning? I only saw him briefly yesterday and we talked about seeing each other this morning but I haven't heard anything. You aren't keeping him locked up, are you?"

"On the contrary, he's keeping himself locked up. Trying to get everything finished up for me. Bless him. I've arranged a generous bonus due to all his hard work. Though I suspect bringing you back home is really the only bonus he needs."

Rosemary blushed and laughed, "I certainly hope so." The day slowly melted away in boxes and trunks, and shy moments between Ophelia and Anthony now that they could be more open in her presence. Watching their happiness was almost more than Rosemary could bear. It seemed far too wonderful.

The sun was low in the sky when Rosemary left Ophelia's, pieces of her hair falling out of pins and dust marks on her shirt. But much of it was now finished. And in that, there was a great deal of contentment. She left the piles of trunks behind, all marked for delivery to Rome, and tiredly walked toward the guest house, having still not heard anything from Donald and desperately needing one of his hugs.

She was surprised to find all the lights in the guest house off, and the car gone. It was possible he'd gone for a drive, or perhaps to the diner, needing a break. She mused on it as she turned back toward the main house and made her way to her own car. She didn't like the empty feeling that was beginning to creep in from the edges of her stomach. For it hadn't truly been long since she'd seen him, and he'd been hard at work. The last thing Rosemary wanted was to make him feel as though she were clinging too fiercely to him.

By the time she reached home, she had been mostly successful at brushing away her thoughts and received a smile from her mother as she walked into the house. It seemed she looked just as disheveled as she felt.

"You've been hard at work today," June said, wiping dust from Rosemary's cheek. "Is Ophelia ready to leave us for good, then?"

"Oh, you mustn't say it like that," she answered tiredly as they walked up the stairs. "I'll miss her too much as it is." It was strange now, to be the one keeping Ophelia's secret, but nevertheless necessary. No matter how her parents had long thought of Ophelia as their own.

"We all will, darling," June answered, following Rosemary into her room. She began turning down the bed as Rosemary went to wash her face and brush her hair, both of them weaving carefully through Rosemary's own boxes and trunks. Gratefully, there were far fewer than those that belonged to her friend, but then again, she wasn't moving an entire home.

"She wants to come and say goodbye before she leaves," Rosemary called to her mother. "Maybe we should throw a small party for her."

"Your father and I were just talking about that today," June agreed. "We'd love to, and something perfectly acceptable can be put together on short notice. Then we'll all go our separate ways, I suppose." She said it so forlornly that Rosemary couldn't help but be sad, and she hugged her mother fiercely.

"You shouldn't talk about it that way."

"Oh, there's nothing to be sad about, really." June blinked back tears and cupped Rosemary's cheek.

"Everybody is so happy. Everything that is happening is so wonderfully *good*. And very deserved."

Twenty-Five

They planned Ophelia's party for two days later. It was to be a very small gathering with all of their favorite foods from over the years. A celebration of time together more than a farewell, they decided. As Rosemary helped plan it, she couldn't help but wish that Anthony could attend. She couldn't wait for the day when she would visit them in Rome and get to see them out and about as a real couple. Showing the entire world their happiness. It would be truly breathtaking.

Donald telephoned early in the morning the day of the party, his voice sleepy. It was the first time she'd heard from him since he'd come to help her pack—though she tried to reign in her excitement at hearing his voice again.

"Good morning," he said, his voice endearingly scratchy.

"Good morning," she answered, her voice equally tired. "It's so good to hear your voice. Does this mean you've finally finished everything?" He chuckled and sighed.

"Yes. It does. I've never felt a bigger sense of accomplishment. Ophelia is officially ready to move to Rome for her happily ever after."

"Oh, good." Rosemary leaned her head against the back of the armchair drowsily, "I'm proud of you."

"Thank you," he responded. "I'll come by early for the party, all right? I've got to finish up packing."

"Do you need my help?"

"No, I'll be okay. I'll see you tonight."

"I love you, Donald." She sat in the armchair for some time after clicking the telephone back into place, her arms folded tightly across her chest. The morning sun was just barely illuminating the edges of the curtains, not quite bright enough yet to make shadows behind all the boxes and trunks.

She thought briefly about joining her family for breakfast, but instead telephoned the kitchen and requested a tea tray which appeared only moments later. Their cook had also included a raspberry pastry, just like the kind she remembered loving from her visits to London. It was a welcome gift. After stirring in the cream and sugar, she raised her saucer to the boxes and trunks, "To the future Mrs. Jones."

Rosemary got ready in Hazel's room that night. Partly to shake up their routine and partly because there wasn't enough space in her room for their normal getting ready shenanigans. And besides all that, there was only one dress left that Rosemary hadn't worn or packed away, so there was no way for her younger sister to help her in that department.

"Let me choose your dress instead," Rosemary requested, setting her things on the divan in the corner of Hazel's room. Her younger sister rarely used it for much other than a place to put things. It was covered in novels and books about horses, her riding hat, and a pair of boots she had insisted on polishing herself. She rarely let anybody touch her riding gear.

"All right, but nothing too childish," Hazel said, putting a Dean Martin record on the turntable. "And nothing blue. I've worn so much blue this season, I could die. And you're wearing blue so I'll let you have that realm all to yourself."

Rosemary's dress was, in fact, a deep turquoise with a flowing skirt that kissed the floor. The neck was high and elegant, and the sleeves ended right at the edge of her shoulder. The top layer of chiffon was delicately formed and embroidered with flowers. She'd be pairing it with simple diamond earrings and a bracelet. Elegant but not dramatic.

"How about this one?" Rosemary brought out a gown the color of a sunset that Hazel had never even seemed to touch. She glanced and it briefly and nodded.

"It will do, I suppose. But no pearls." Hazel's voice was suddenly stern and it made Rosemary laugh as she laid both of their gowns out on the bed.

"All right, no pearls. I'll also remember that for my wedding."

"Yes, please do." They laughed together and sat at the vanity, brushing on powder and carefully applying lipstick.

Hazel surprised her by asking for help with her hair. It wasn't something she really needed help with, but Rosemary had a feeling it was more of a sentimental request than anything. Though Hazel would surely never admit it. Rosemary helped put soft curls in her sister's hair, which she kept quite long. When they finished, it was absolutely incredible.

"Mother and Dad are going to have to build a fence around you, Hazel," Rosemary teased, turning her attention to her own curls. Hazel blushed but didn't say anything as she took a few pins in her hands and helped her sister twist the front pieces of her hair back.

"There," Hazel said proudly as she finished, "now we'll both be the talk of the town." They had only just finished getting ready, laughing far too loudly at their own foolish jokes, when June entered the room

"Oh, good, you're ready," she said, holding them at arm's length. "And you look absolutely lovely. Both of you. Rosemary, Donald just pulled up in the drive. I assume Ophelia isn't far behind."

Rosemary shot them a smile before rushing out of the room and down the stairs. "Don't ruin your hair!" Hazel called after her, her teasing tone very evident. Rosemary just laughed and resisted the urge to slide down the banister of the staircase, which would've been faster, eventually making it out the front door. She saw him some ways down the drive, leaning against the car. Probably waiting for her. He always did that before they walked inside together. She smiled and tried to calm down, though every urge she had begged her to run straight into his arms.

As she got closer to him, her shoes crunching on the gravel, she began to notice that he wasn't dressed for the evening. He was wearing a suit, but not one meant for a dinner party. It was his business suit. The one he traveled in. But surely he hadn't forgotten about the party? He was leaning against the car, arms folded, eyes glued to the ground. As she drew closer and he heard her footsteps, his gaze pulled up toward hers. It was like running into a wall.

Something was wrong. A darkness she couldn't match grew from the shadows of uncertainty and became the only thing she could see. It choked her. And every instinct she had began screaming in response, urging her to fight it. Urging her to grab that connection between them and hold onto it with every piece of strength she possessed. But it wasn't there. She couldn't find it. Try as she might to reach him through the darkness, she couldn't get past the wall.

The last steps toward him were torture until she was close enough to see his eyes. But the deep gaze she knew so well, the gaze so full of love and certainty, was either completely empty or utterly caved in. She didn't know which was worse.

"What's going on?" She said the words but it wasn't her voice.

"Rosemary, I just…" He had broken their gaze and couldn't look at her as he began talking. No, he *wouldn't* look at her. "I can't do it. I just can't do this."

When Rosemary had been very little, she'd gone swimming somewhere with her mother and father. Hazel hadn't even been born yet. She couldn't remember where they'd gone. She only remembered jumping from a high place and landing in the freezing water, coming up laughing beside her father. But there was no laughing this time. There was no breaking above the water.

"What?" Speaking hurt. Each word ripped from her throat. "What are you talking about? Why? What's happened?" Behind her eyes tearing began building. Tears so hot with confusion that they burned. She couldn't see him around them. Only the outline of him refusing to look at her.

"I can't." It was all he would say, in a voice so soft, she could barely hear.

"That's not good enough!" She clenched her fists and dashed the tears from her cheeks. Everything burned. The tears. The words. "Tell me what's going on! Talk to me. Please. What has happened? *How* is this happening?"

"*I can't!*" He gripped her arms tightly, and even being that close, there was nothing in his eyes. "I can't do this, and I can't explain why. I'm leaving. Tonight." His voice was tight with emotion he didn't dare feel, and she angrily shoved him away because of it. But when they separated, he took everything inside of her with him.

"I don't understand!" She buried her face in her hands, tugged at her hair. But her voice came out in a feverish wail. "*Please, Donald.* Please. Just tell me what is happening. I love you! You love me! We both know that this is right. Just talk to me and we'll figure things out. I promise." But he was even further away now, retreating steadily behind his wall. He clearly refused to look at her. Even took a few steps away. His eyes had caved in. And all of it had landed on her.

He was running. Plain and simple, he was running. Running from the uncertainties, running from the truth, running from happiness. Running because it was easier. A darkness had been lurking behind them, growing in the unknowns, and rather than fight it with her, he was shoving it all away.

"Rosemary, you'll find somebody so...*so* much better than me." He clenched his fists and turned back to face her. "You deserve so much better."

"I don't *want* anybody else!" If the end of the world had had a sound, it would've been the anguish in her voice. "Why are you doing this? I don't understand!" He was silent. Silent like a tomb, buried in stone. But she was the one on the inside. She looked then into the eyes of the man she loved and couldn't find him there. And she knew that this was goodbye. And that was too simple.

It didn't matter that everything inside of her cried out for her to fight. It didn't matter that it was the only thing she'd ever been absolutely certain of. It didn't matter that it had been right. So right. Because she couldn't touch him. He was gone. He'd already left.

Twenty-Six

Rome, Italy
Winter 1954

The grapes had long since been harvested by the time Rosemary arrived at the vineyard. Trailing behind Anthony and Ophelia, just outside the orb of their happiness, she listened to Signore Alfonso explaining the harvesting process and could only think that it was somehow fitting it was all over. Soon he would take them to a room in his villa and they would gather around to try the wine itself, and Ophelia would thank her friend for his hospitality in showing them around his property. And perhaps he'd wink and say, "Anything for the daughter of my dear friend. May you find happiness here, *cara mia*."

In the meantime, Rosemary was content to follow at the back of the group and breathe in the filtered sunlight. It wasn't a cloudy day, but it somehow seemed as though a thin piece of fabric had been stretched across the sun. She plunged her hands deep in her pockets to ward off the chill of the breeze, one lock of hair blowing into her eyes as she did so.

"Cold, Rosemary?" Anthony asked, looking back to check on her. She didn't miss the concern ringing the edges of his dark eyes. Only wished that it didn't have to be for her.

"No, I'm fine, thank you," she answered quickly, brushing off the thought that she was always cold these days. He gave her a quick, warm smile before turning back to their lively host who was now leading them toward his home.

The toast went exactly as Rosemary had predicted, and the consistency of that settled comfortably inside of her. Signore Alfonso had brought them into his personal study for the toast, where the walls were lined with books and one window spanned the back wall. Rosemary was sure the view was lovely in the summer. But now it looked over the empty vineyard and the thin sun rather bleakly. She swirled the wine around in her glass for just a moment before taking a thoughtful sip. If not for the presence of it in her glass, she might have been tempted to believe that the vineyard always looked like this.

"Miss Covington," Signore Alfonso approached her with his soft but warm presence, "how are you enjoying Italy?"

"Very much, thank you," she responded, a small but genuine smile spreading across her face. "I've always adored Rome, and your vineyard is lovely."

"Ah, *grazie, mi bella*," he answered with a soft chuckle. "It is kind of you to say it. You enjoy our history, yes? Ophelia tells me you are a student of the past."

"I try to be."

"Then you must visit my chapel." His response was immediate as he gestured out the window. "Just on the edge of the vineyard." Rosemary followed the path of his gesture and took in the small chapel that peaked through the various rows of branches, and couldn't help it that her curiosity was provoked.

"An interesting place for a chapel," she commented lightly. "How old is it?"

"Oh, it is new," he answered, and for a moment, his eyes darkened a bit. "I built it after the war. There were too many churches surrounding us that had been destroyed. I wanted to remind myself, my family, and the people who depend on our vineyard that there is life after destruction."

"Do you believe in God, Signore?" She wondered this aloud after admiring the building for a moment, which made his eyes begin gleaming again.

"We all believe in something. But even if it is different for you, the chapel is a special place. Go see it if only to admire the stained glass."

The chapel was bigger up close. Rosemary stood outside and admired it for several moments, taking in the old architecture. Clearly, Signore Alfonso had designed it to mimic the greater cathedrals in Rome and beyond, and she liked the idea. She imagined what the people here must have seen only very recently, all the horrors of war, and was touched at the idea of building such a place so soon afterward.

One of the large double doors swung open easily at her touch, letting in a shaft of the watered-down sun onto clean stone floors. She closed it firmly behind her, allowing her eyes to adjust to the jewel-colored light inside. Signore Alfonso hadn't been lying: the stained glass was beautiful. It filled the back wall of the chapel behind the altar and depicted the healing of a woman. The figure of Jesus was crouched down next to her, with a hand on her shoulder as if to heal her soul as well. It was rather intimate for a stained glass window, and Rosemary had to wonder if it had really happened that way.

She approached the altar, walking past several rows of neat wooden benches, and tried not to make small tapping noises with her shoes as she did so. Even if the chapel was empty, there was a sense of reverence in it, of a respect deserved. She brushed past the altar, which was a beautiful dark wood overlaid with red velvet, and toward a wrought iron stand which held candles in various stages of life.

One candle at the top of the stand stood unburned, ready for a fresh prayer. But Rosemary didn't light that one. Instead, she set the flame to one near the middle of the stand, the wax melted unevenly. And the words to her prayer didn't formulate in her heart as she did so, but merely gathered together in a feeling that she sent toward the stained glass and beyond.

"Do you light a candle for yourself, Signora?" Somehow the voice that spoke then didn't startle Rosemary, though she hadn't heard anybody enter the chapel. She turned from the candles to see a man, older than Signore Alfonso, dressed in the clean but serviceable clothes of a field worker. Rosemary briefly wondered how long he had been working here at this very vineyard.

"No, Signore," she answered, shaking her head and standing aside so he could light one himself. "Do you?" He didn't answer at first. Only lit the fresh candle, closed his eyes briefly, and then turned to her with smiling blue eyes.

"No." His answer was simple but pleasant as he settled next to her on the front bench. They sat in a rather companionable silence for a long while, absorbing the quiet and serenity surrounding them. And after some time, Rosemary thought that he was about to get up and leave without another word. Instead, he turned slightly toward her. "What happened to him, Signora? The one you light candles for?"

Rosemary couldn't help it that her fists clenched tightly then—so tightly that her nails dug into her skin painfully. But that was nothing compared to what slipped out of its precarious cage inside her heart. No, nothing in the world compared to that. She'd learned that quickly. "He left." The old, blue eyes looked at her thoughtfully for several long moments, and Rosemary was surprised when a light sheen of moisture eventually gathered in their corners.

"*Ma ti ha amato molto.*" But he loved you very much.

Rosemary pressed her eyes closed at this and cursed the way that they burned. "He did tell me so," she whispered, "but people lie." He squeezed her hands lightly, only then alerting her to the fact that he had smoothed them out and now held them gently.

"I do not think it was a lie." His voice was low and comforting, tugging mercilessly at the cage she'd fought so valiantly to build. "You don't believe that either. That is why you light candles."

"I *want* to not believe it. I want to believe so many things about it all."

"And what stops you, Signora?"

"Reality." Her voice was bleak, but even that was more hospitable than the landscape inside her. "The daily truth I wake up to now. I tried so hard to believe that something else existed. And for just a moment, it did. But even the exception doesn't last." She couldn't tell if anything she said made sense, mostly because she was battling complete numbness and the never-ending tide of black despair. But he seemed to absorb it all well enough.

"Something lives on inside of you that is much stronger than all of that," he finally concluded. "*Speranza.* Hope. It has revived many dying flowers."

She chose to believe him then, mostly because she didn't have the heart to tell him that she didn't think anything lived inside her anymore. She merely smiled as best she could. Taking comfort in his clear eyes and the wisdom in his words. He returned her smile and lifted her hands to his lips, kissing them softly.

"May God bless you, Signora." He stood slowly and turned back toward the door, his movements slow but sure as he retreated from the sanctuary. He stopped suddenly and faced her once more, a question in his eyes. "Did you love him?"

"More than anything." And even through the thick tears, she could see the smile he beamed at her.

Twenty-Seven

Rome, Italy
February 1955

Ophelia was more beautiful than any bride had a right to be. Walking down the aisle of a small chapel somewhere in the streets of Rome, her smile was brighter than any strand of diamonds. Her dress was almost too white. She seemed to carry an angelic aura around her all day, but especially as she approached the altar where Anthony waited with tears streaming down his face. Rosemary couldn't decide if she should hand him her handkerchief from where she stood ready to take the bouquet, as it was already soaked with her own tears.

It would've been like Ophelia to tease them a bit about their state of emotions once she arrived at the altar, but instead, her smile grew as she handed Rosemary the beautiful array of yellow roses. Her light blue eyes were brilliant in a sheen of tears that had yet to fall as she kissed Rosemary's cheek and turned back to face her groom. At that moment, it didn't matter at all that the chapel wasn't full to the brim with people. It was so full of their love that there was hardly room for anything else. Rosemary thought they might all burst with it.

And for the rest of the day, Ophelia and Anthony were the only two people on the Earth. All through the parties and dancing and laughing that filled the rest of the day, they had eyes only for each other. Back at the villa, with the sun striking every surface and music filling in whatever it missed, Rosemary watched them through the festivities and could hardly bear the happiness she felt for them. It had never been more deserved by anybody. She drank in every detail of it, every sound and smell and the taste of the food. She'd have to write to her family about it later, yes, but it was also something joyful. A promise kept. And in that was a hope that Rosemary needed more than she needed air.

The Covingtons had been unable to make it to the wedding. Ophelia had told Arnold and June about the marriage after she had arrived with Anthony in Rome. It had come as a shock, but mostly they had accepted it with grace. June had been more willing, and Arnold a bit more hesitant. They all knew it was because he felt more responsibility for Ophelia than he'd ever let on. He had been so close to her father.

But despite this, they had sent their best wishes and endless amounts of love. Though they couldn't attend the wedding itself, Rosemary knew they'd be expecting a detailed report of it as soon as she could get it to them. It was enough to tempt her into jotting it down in a notebook. *But no*, she decided with a slight shake of her head. *If even for just this moment, I'll try and be fully present. No hiding in my mind today.*

Ophelia and Anthony danced the night away, seeming to never tire as the music kept going and going. They would leave the next morning for Florence to begin the first leg of their honeymoon, and then on to France. Rosemary was leaving the next day as well, off to London to begin her new job. But again, she wasn't going to think about that. She would only drink in the happiness of her dearest friend and be grateful for every ounce of it. Watching them together that evening, their dreams finally a reality, Rosemary could almost believe that there had never been two people more in love.

She was very suddenly jerked from these thoughts, however, as Ophelia pulled her out onto the dance floor to the tune of something very Italian and vitally happy.

"You are the epitome of all that a bride should be," Rosemary said. "Grace Kelly herself couldn't have done it any better."

Ophelia laughed, "Coming from you, I understand just how valuable those words are. Thank you." They whirled around a few more minutes until they were laughing too hard to continue, eventually landing in a corner somewhere trying to fix one another's hair.

"I doubt I'll get to talk with you again for quite some time," Rosemary said then, saying what they were both trying to avoid. "But I can't wait to hear absolutely everything. You'll find a way to call at least once?"

"It's a promise," Ophelia said, squeezing her hands. And for just one moment, she forgot she was a bride on the happiest day of her life and let her eyes soften in concern. "Is there anything I can do for you? You've done so much for us."

"We both know you've done more for me than I could ever repay you for." Rosemary felt her voice becoming businesslike. But that wasn't a surprise. It was her newest way of controlling everything that went on underneath the surface. "But there's a letter on your desk with a United States address. When you get home, could you send it for me? I don't think I can. Writing it was hard enough."

"Consider it done." Ophelia kissed her cheek. "Enjoy London, dear. It's going to be spectacular. Give my love to your uncle."

Ophelia had the letter sent the next morning before she and Anthony departed in a shiny car trailing tin cans behind it. But Rosemary didn't know that. She simply waved her farewell and smiled, practically aching in her happiness for them.

She went back inside for only a few moments to finish her breakfast. She drank the last of her aromatic coffee in silence and went for one more look around the house. Just to thank it one last time for cradling her heart until it felt patched up enough to do the rest itself. That seemed to be the job of this remarkable place: to take things that were broken and make something beautiful from the cracked colors. It hadn't completely worked on her, but it had tried. And that was enough.

A car arrived for her shortly thereafter to take her to the airport. Its windows weren't as shiny and it had no cans trailing behind it to bounce happily on the Roman streets. But it was a car taking her forward. And again Rosemary had to be content that that was enough. It was an attitude she'd had to develop in order to survive. Because that was all Rosemary Covington did anymore and in fact, all she expected to ever do again. Survive.

The letter smelled like roses and faraway places. Next to the stamps from Rome was his name, written in her unmistakable hand. He pulled out the slightly yellow pages carefully. They were thick and promising, just the way she liked stationary. He wondered where it had come from. A small shop somewhere in Rome, probably. He could imagine what the outing had been like, what she might have worn. How she might have looked. It was all much too real before his eyes. He could even hear her laugh, perhaps how it would've sounded as she talked with the shopkeeper. And all of that before he had even unfolded the paper.

There were tear streaks on the pages, and the penmanship was shaky. It made him wonder how long it had been between writing the letter and actually posting it. The words themselves seemed far off at first. But that was because the letter contained the last vestiges of a soul sent away in the post.

Dear Donald,

I'm not sure if you'll ever get this letter. I still haven't decided if I'll send it. But Ophelia won't quit nagging me about writing down everything I'm feeling. So to appease her, I'm doing this. We're in Rome now. I tried not to let her take me along, but you know her.

There came a point when I couldn't be around my family anymore, as much as I love them. It became much too painful when I had to begin facing how excited they had been to have you as a son and brother. I had to distance myself from them, as silly or pathetic as that might sound. Perhaps both. But no matter how it sounds, it was the truth, and because of it, Ophelia packed me up along with her things and took me to Italy. She wouldn't dream of leaving me alone.

Things have gotten more manageable, though, and my family is too good for words. I think they understood why it was that way long before I ever did. There were so many days when I couldn't even look at Hazel and didn't know why. It wasn't until later that I realized it was because we'd been together, watching her ride, the day I realized I loved you. Not that it was her fault, because it wasn't. It was nobody's fault, I think. In any case, they are all excited for the new changes in my life. Some days, I think that they only know how to love.

My bedroom here in Rome is small and overlooks the courtyard. Which is full of rose bushes. Mostly yellow ones. Those are Ophelia's favorite. We've been planning the wedding constantly. It'll be in early February.

Truthfully, I didn't know a person could hurt like that and live. I didn't know emptiness like that existed. I didn't know you could break that wide open and still look whole on the outside. I've experienced hurt. Deep hurts. You know that. And because of the depth of those hurts, I somehow believed that nothing could ever hurt that badly again. I thought I'd be strong enough to be whole through any other pain. But I was wrong. Nothing ever hurt like this did. But that was always a pattern with you, I suppose. You were always proving that you were the exception to every rule.

There are a million things that I wish. And a million things I've cried into my pillow every night. But now that I'm sitting here, writing something you'll potentially read, I'm not sure what to do about all of them. I'll tell you a few truths, though.

The truth is that something like this is so much more than you think it is when you see others experience it. It is so much more than losing the person you love more than anything in this world. That in itself is a tragedy too deep to explain.

But more than this, it is the loss of a dream. At least, it was for me. It was the loss of something I had secretly hoped for my entire life. Prayed for. Waited for. Longed for. Underneath all the pain life handed me, it was the only thing I really wanted. I wanted life to prove me wrong, and for the briefest of brilliant moments, it did. But if all of those losses are added together, it is a miracle that anybody has ever survived it. That's the key, though, I've discovered. Survival. Pure and simple survival.

I spent a great deal of time throwing things away. I was unaware I had such vehemence inside of me. But so many things found their way to the trash. Anything that reminded me of you. Dresses, ticket stubs, blankets, and books. Yes, even books. Hugo. And even some Fitzgerald. I hadn't wanted Fitzgerald to be right. I thought that we had proven him wrong.

Ophelia kept a bottle of whiskey in her home just for me. Even though I hadn't touched it in years, she always said she wanted it on hand "just in case." We drank it together those first few days. In fact, we drank more than one bottle. Sitting on the floor in her bedroom in Newport, we drank whiskey until we couldn't see. For days we did this. And we listened to Frank Sinatra until we ruined the record.

And like the fool that I am, I thought that these things would make it better. But when I finally emerged from the stupor, I had to face the reality that nothing really can.

I wanted to be angry, but when the time came to feel that emotion, it didn't last long. It's a pity, too, because anger is easier to feel than everything else. But I couldn't be mad at you. Not for long. Not when I know you so well. Not when I sensed the anguish you were feeling, and that you thought you were doing the right thing.

I could never say that it was the right thing, but it was clear you thought it was. You thought it was the only option. And there's something to that. But maybe I'm rambling now. I'm having a hard time deciding if there was a point to writing this.

After the wedding, I'm moving to London. I have a job lined up and I'm as excited as I can be. My uncle is so excited that sometimes I think he'll burst. He has a childlike quality I've always admired. He's got all sorts of things planned for us to do. I think he sometimes forgets that I'll be working.

I'll say it the only way I know how to. Honestly. That was a trait I was once proud of, I think. Sometimes, I'm not quite sure who I used to be before you. There are a lot of things that have been wiped from my memory. A lot of things I have to be reminded of. I also wasn't aware that grief could do that. Make you forget things.

I wish that you had remembered. I know it sounds foolish, as I sit here admitting that I am having a hard time remembering things. But it's true. It's the only thing I really know to be true anymore. I wish that you had remembered the first time you held my hand. Or the first time you kissed me. Or the day we realized we loved each other. I wish you had remembered the rightness and decided that the rightness was worth pushing through the unknowns for.

But maybe you did remember. Maybe you still do. I know that I do. No matter what memories grief has stolen from me, there are some moments that will remain on my heart forever. I've mentioned a few. They are never far from me, these moments. Sometimes, in fact, I have to make them leave or I'll simply sit and remember all day. Playing them over and over again as if that could make them come back to life.

I'm not sure how I want to end this letter you may or may not read. Or if there was even a point in telling you any of these truths. For all I know, if I do send this letter, you'll get it and never read it. You may throw it away. Just like I threw so many things away. And I couldn't blame you for that.

But I knew you better than anybody, and you knew me. There was a connection between us so strong that it overwhelmed me at times. Sometimes I imagine that I can still feel it, across all the distance that separates us. But maybe that's just foolish. And maybe time will eventually pull it to shreds. Maybe then it would finally stop hurting.

I'm not exactly sure. I thought once that it might stop hurting, but I don't think that's a truth. I think it becomes easier to get out of bed in the morning and continue moving forward. I think you get better at pretending to go on with your life. But some pain doesn't really go away. Especially when there's no way to know for sure, no way to really fix it.

Believe me, I tried everything I could think of to fix it, and nothing worked. Not one thing.

But then again, none of those things were you. And after knowing what it was like to be loved by you, I can't blame my heart for refusing to be comforted by anything else.

I'm going to go give this letter to Ophelia now. I think she and Anthony are having their tea downstairs. Though I can hear her laughing, so maybe I'll wait. At some point, she'll want to read it and approve of this step I've taken. I'll never be quite sure if I did anything to deserve her. She's so happy here, Donald. It would make you happy to see it. She and Anthony are so perfect together. It is so right. So obvious it hurts. We knew that feeling once.

Love,
Rosemary

Twenty-Eight

London, England
Spring 1955

It was a foggy day in London, several months after Rosemary's arrival. She looked out of the window of her office and smiled at the street below her. It was made of stones and held cars snuggly against the curbs. The clouds hung low across the tops of the buildings and promised that it would rain soon. Not uncommon for London, but somehow it seemed more fitting today. She thought she'd be able to finish up her articles early and make it home in time for tea. Uncle Louis had plans for a play that evening, and it had been ages since she'd been to the theater.

She sat back down at her typewriter and looked over her notes once again. She was working on a piece about veterans of the war, and while it might have been disheartening, there was also hope in that. Ten years after the war, wounds were deep as ever. Rosemary liked to believe that by taking articles like these, she could somehow help the country heal. It might not have been realistic, but she needed to believe in something.

She clacked at her typewriter for an hour or so longer, just enough to get the bulk of the article on paper before blowing the ink dry. It was one of three she was currently working on, and all three of them needed heavy editing that evening in order to meet her deadline. But in her experience, such editing was best done at their home on the West End. With a good cup of tea and music playing from the turntable.

"Miss Covington?" A sharp knock came sounding from the glass window in her office door, and Ethel stepped through. She was a darling British woman with soft brown hair and moss green eyes. She worked as the secretary for most of them.

"Yes, Ethel?" Rosemary finished blowing the ink dry and began putting all her papers in order.

"Are you leaving for the day?"

"Yes. Why?"

"Oh, well, a package just arrived for you. I wasn't sure if you just wanted to leave it until tomorrow. It could be something pertaining to your articles." It wasn't uncommon, especially with the people Rosemary consulted. Her journeys to find information were often adventurous. And usually ended in her receiving a package or two from all kinds of crowds: wealthy people with titles or shopkeepers. It would be a book or old newspaper or family journal she always made sure to return after use. Rosemary's first urge was to leave it for the next day, but something nagged at her that she might need it for her editing that evening.

"Bring it in for me if you would." Ethel reappeared several moments later, handing her a small package wrapped in brown paper. It was obviously a book. But there was nothing on it. Nothing to indicate where it might have come from, or who it had been delivered to for that matter. It didn't even have her name on it. Rosemary's brow furrowed as she tore the paper away.

"Ethel!" She grabbed her purse and coat and ran out the door, "Where did this come from? Who brought it?" Ethel looked so shocked that she couldn't answer, and Rosemary didn't have time. She simply turned and fled. "I'll finish my articles tomorrow! I'll see you then!"

"What is it?" Ethel called.

"It's a Hugo!"

The fog made it hard for the cab driver to go any faster, and his thick eyebrows drew together in displeasure as Rosemary kept urging him forward.

"Westminster Abbey, please! Please drive faster!"

"It may take a few more minutes in this fog, miss. I'm sorry." He sounded polite for how irritated she knew she was making him. But that hardly mattered.

"Oh, never mind that." She threw a wad of bills into his lap and jumped out of the door. Her coat flew out behind her as she ran, and her heels made sharp cracking noises on the stones. She hugged the book to her chest and ran as fast as she could, shocking more than one British gentleman ambling along the sidewalk.

The abbey rose from the fog sharply, beautiful in the gloom. Any other day, she would've been delighted to go inside and light a candle. It was a good day for prayers. But she stopped at the wrought iron gate, clutching it and panting. She looked about wildly, but she couldn't see far in the fog. She started walking toward the doors of the abbey once she'd caught her breath but stopped quite suddenly when the mist finally pulled back enough to reveal a lone figure standing on the grass. Looking up at the ancient building as though soaking it all in. She approached slowly, and when she stopped next to him, her mind was blank in disbelief and fear. He turned to her and looked at the book in her hand.

"I always knew that you'd never read it."

"How?" She was incredulous, and it made him laugh. That sound alone had the power to break everything inside of her all over again. Once it had had the power to do the opposite. Back when it had promised safe things. When she'd thought promises were easy to keep.

"Because I know you better than anybody."

She took a shaky breath and gestured toward the abbey, "What do you think?"

"It's just as beautiful as you said it was," he answered, and the sound of his voice distracted her from the fact that her insides felt raw and unsteady. She finally dared to look over at him again. He looked well, for the most part. But something was different.

Tentatively, she let out a long breath and tried to reach out to him. Just a bit, with her heart. To see if she could still feel what he felt, and terrified that she'd find the impenetrable wall there once again. But there was no wall. It was different inside his heart, though. A bit colder, a bit lonelier. Harsher, maybe. And broken. Though perhaps stronger, too, above it all.

"Donald, why are you here?" She would never know where she got the strength to ask him that. Her heart was pounding so hard that she could barely hear her own voice over it. He turned from looking at the abbey and faced her, taking his hands from his pockets. Though he didn't reach out to her.

"I came to do what Frank Sinatra couldn't."

"What?" It was almost enough to make her laugh.

"I came to get the woman I love."

Rosemary wanted to laugh then, but tears fell instead. "And...what if it's too late to fix everything? What if there's no hope?"

"I don't believe that's possible. Not with us. Not with this," he said and then drew an unsteady breath. "But if you truly feel that way, then I'll stop for a drink before I fly home."

A deep silence stretched before them as tears continued to fall down Rosemary's cheeks. And part of her wanted to turn and run. Part of her was too frightened to let the pain out in the open and try and fix it. Forgiveness had been easy. Trust was another thing entirely. And part of her was much too broken to ever hope for healing. But her own words came back to her mind then. *I wish you had remembered the rightness and decided that the rightness was worth pushing through the unknowns for.*

"I'm so scared, Donald." His eyes softened to a place she remembered all too well, and when he pulled her close, it was there. Somehow, someway, through everything. It was still there.

Safety. He pressed a soft kiss to her forehead.

"We'll be brave together." His voice was tentative, well aware of the shattering point, but strong. Like a hope. And somehow that was better than a promise.

Epilogue

Dear Ophelia,

Thank you so much for sending the photographs of little Melody. She's absolutely lovely. Donald and I are smitten. We're hoping to be able to come and visit you before she gets too old. What a joy it must be to have her, and to get to hold her in your arms. I know you're already the most spectacular mother. And I'm sure Anthony is overjoyed. Please continue to send pictures as often as you can, and even the smallest update. Donald and I want to be as involved with Melody's life as possible.

I've included some pictures of our new flat, and you'll find that we, too, have a new arrival. His name is George. He was a birthday present from Donald, and I'm absolutely thrilled. He always had a dog growing up, so it was a special thing for him to be able to bring George home.

It is still strange to me that we are here in London. Living here this past year has been a dream come true. We've had so many ups and downs, of which you're fully aware I know, that it has been such a beautiful thing to live in so much joy. When Donald told me that his firm wanted to open a branch in London, I was speechless. It all seemed much too good to be true, especially after he showed up in London on that foggy day.

For such a long time it was so hard, Ophelia. I waited for months and months for him to leave again. I avoided talking about it to people. I avoided collecting things from our time together. I always thought, "It will be less to throw away later." And to be completely honest, I wasn't always sure. There were moments when it seemed that perhaps he had done the right thing before, leaving as he had. There was even one moment when we did fall apart again. And I wasn't surprised. And as strange as this sounds, it didn't hurt. Not one bit. It burned like a strange, icy fire inside my chest, and then all of a sudden, it was cooled. And I felt strangely free. And I knew that we loved each other more than either of us could say and that a connection like that isn't explainable or always simple. It exists even when we aren't together, this unbreakable cord that somehow lives between us.

Donald is a very complicated man. I've known that since the moment I met him at your party all that time ago. He gets so afraid of things. And life chases him around so much. The hardest thing for me to try and understand was his will to fight. Sometimes it seems as though he stops fighting in the moments when fighting is the most crucial. But I think this is me being unfair. The truth is that life is complicated, love is complicated, and it takes time to put things in order. It takes time to align our hearts and minds and put them in the right place for our own lives. I think you and Anthony understand that better than anybody.

And so unsurprisingly here we are, in our very own flat in London. The strange thing is that anything would have seemed right. If I'd never seen Donald again, I still would have known that he loved me, and I him. And until my very last breath, I would have felt that connection from my heart to his. And I would have had a beautiful and completely happy life. Because I finally realized that the key to my freedom was my own heart all along. I finally discovered that I was enough for every moment and every darkness. I discovered that some things, like love like this, always live on and exist in your heart no matter what happens. It's just the way it is.

George is by the radiator on a mat Donald bought for him, sleeping the day away. Donald will probably work a bit late. He's very excited about the opening of the new branch. He's been working tirelessly. I have started writing fewer articles for the paper, which is news you'll be excited to hear because I have done this so that I can start work on a novel. Donald has been so supportive. At the end of each day, he tells me about how the branch is progressing and I talk him through my ideas. We sometimes do this over tea, which he is still getting used to. As you can probably imagine, it isn't the idea of food that he's getting used to, but the ritual of it all. Though I'm convinced it's been a charade all along. I see the gleam in his eye as we become more and more British every day.

Thank you again for the pictures of Melody. Kiss her for us and give Anthony our love. I expect this letter will reach you before then, but I eagerly wait for our next call. It will be good to hear your voice.

Love,
Rosemary